# Mystery at the Covington Museum
# "A Knight to Remember"
# The Adventures of Jamie the Kid

# SARAH CHRISTINE ADDAMS

# Index

# Chapter 1

"Come little ones, 'tis far, far better to be inside, than out there on such a day hot as this!"

Jamie couldn't help smiling as the pot bellied man dressed in a leprechaun outfit toddled on by. He was the picture of perfection with his wild orange hair and curly-toed slippers. Striped stockings that pulled tight on his stocky thighs and a velvet green hat completed the look. Leaning over a group of uncertain children who bit their fingers in anticipation he smiled broadly. Gleaming white teeth held an old cob pipe that blew rings of colored smoke around his head.

The museum was hosting a party in honor of St. Patrick's Day and no expense had been spared in order to make certain everything look the part. Green streamers hung from every inch of the ceiling, twisting and dipping down in a playful fashion. Paper bells and pictures of leprechauns colored by the neighboring children were plastered to walls with cheap, milky colored tape. There was even a large bowl filled with green punch and a giant cake with the words, *Happy St. Patty's Day* scrolled across in choppy icing.

Lack of money was always an issue and even with their constant fund raisers they barely managed to keep their doors open. But today was a special day and pennies were pinched until they turned to dust to make it all come together. The mood was friendly but with her impending need not to be noticed, Jamie was on edge.

No fliers had been posted since she went missing from the orphanage. No telegraphs had been sent, no policemen notified. If they were, the first place they would have come looking would have been the museum. It was a place where a lot of people came and went; clean, with facilities. There were more eyes to spot a missing person and get the message out to the public.

It had been a week since her adventure with the pirates. During that time she discovered a crawl space in the attic where she could sleep without fear of being noticed for as long as she wanted. In truth, she hadn't so much discovered it as Jimbo had shown it to her. It was the night after her high seas escapade when the place was closing down for the night. He noticed her hanging around the mounted knights situated in front of a painted, cardboard castle entrance.

"We'll be closing soon miss," he said, eyes downcast as the last bit of mud was sloshed away with his mop.

"Ah, okay." Was all she could muster as she pretended to study the polished marble busts of Socrates and Aristotle.

They were positioned across from the bust of General Custer which seemed to be an odd place to be. After a few moments he stopped mopping and walked to the back of the museum. She followed at a safe distance, not wanting to alert him.

When he disappeared behind heavy, black curtains under a doorway with a sign that read: *Employees Only,* she hesitated. Blending in with the street people on the museum floor was easy enough but surely she would be noticed if she was spotted in the restricted area. Taking a deep breath, she pushed forward, beyond the thick drapes and stumbled forward into a dimly lit room filled with dirty mops, rusty buckets and two sinks so deep she could take a bath in them. It smelled of bleach and a lemony scent of which she was unfamiliar. Back at the orphanage all they had was the cheap, liquid soap that came in the giant plastic bottles to clean with; which made cleaning the mirrors nearly impossible. Luckily, there weren't many.

The naked light bulb flickered overhead giving it the appearance of a haunted house as the strange shapes and sounds began to overtake her. *More like a haunted cell,* she thought, shivering as she remembered all those cold, lonely nights in the bowels of the ship with only the rats to keep her company. She had lost sight of the janitor and as she followed the path covered in soggy boot prints towards a closet at the far end, a soft chirping sound stopped her in her tracks. Turning around slowly she was startled to see him standing there, mop in hand, staring back at her with those sparkling blue eyes.

"Just came back to change out my mop head," he said briskly, as though he was reporting to his boss. Jamie's face turned beet red. She had been caught. And now, all she could do was wait. A small gust of wind blew down on her from the ceiling, causing her to shiver.

"It's the darndest thing. I just can't seem to keep that door locked on the attic. It's a shame really. Someone could sneak in there and set up camp and we'd never know about it; being that no one checks up there and all."

Her head shot straight up when he said that. *A safe place to sleep!* She had never experienced that before. The orphanage was too crowded and the museum was too open. And as the flickering bulb shined on his weathered face, she could swear she saw the makings of a smile quivering across his thin lips. He never asked her what she was doing back there. And as the lights on the main floor were turned off, he walked out of the room, leaving her to her own devices.

Moments later she had fished the twisted metal ladder out of the open closet and was tugging at the pull chord on the attic door. She still had to be careful. Even hidden all the way in the back, the night guard could still hear if something fell. With a terrific creak the door came flying open, along with the attached ladder. Luckily, the ladder was jammed, so she was spared the expense of a concussion. Using all her body weight Jamie managed to dislodge the sliding ladder and climb up before the enormous watchman came in to investigate.

Once inside she had to fight off a multitude of cobwebs and hanging strands of dust before she could find her way forward. It was a rather pleasant cubby hole, just big enough for one person to enjoy. There was an old, gray mattress that had once been white and a tiny window carved in to the thick boarded wall. It seemed like an afterthought, being so small and high up. Not even a full grown man standing on his tip toes could reach it to see out.

The room was unusually cool and as her teeth began to chatter she wondered if this was such a good idea after all. The main floor was more open but at least it was warmer. And then, as her eyes adjusted to the darkness, she noticed a large lump in the corner. Her heart stopped. *Was it an animal? Or maybe another person who had figured out the room was unlocked?* With a trembling heart she decided to investigate. After being stuck aboard a ship full of angry pirates, all of whom wanted to kill her, there wasn't anything she couldn't handle.

Sticking out her foot, she nudged it gently at first. If it was something that meant to do her harm there would be some distance between them. Nothing happened. Growing bolder, she grabbed it, wrestling it to the ground like an attacker. She had gotten pretty good at wrestling. Being bullied as much as she was by the other girls in the children's home was made her a strong fighter.

A big cloud of dust emerged from the soft, lumpy creature, causing her to cough uncontrollably. In a mad frenzy she ripped it open, grunting like a wild animal in heat. A blanket, full of dust bunnies and balled up cobwebs, but a blanket none the less emerged from her iron grip. There was some sort of pattern dotting what was once a pristine covering for someone far wealthier than she. Rubbing the frayed material against her cheek, Jamie could almost picture the smiling parents as they hovered above their sleeping child, tucking the edges of the thick quilt around their tiny body. Never would they know hunger or rejection. Only love and praise for their good works would be permitted to be spoken in that house full of love.

Salty tears trickled down the end of her nose, tucking up inside her nostril, tickling her hairs. *Someday that will be me*, she vowed silently as she settled in for the night. *Someday I will be happy too.* Every night since then she slept up in the attic. Jimbo was kind enough to leave the light on for her in the backroom so she could see what she was doing. It was a safe place, but very lonely. On the main floor she felt at home with the wax figures and misshapen props hovering around her to keep her company. Up there she was all alone—alone in a dark, empty room.

But as the sunlight bounced off the shiny, gold handled doors she was reminded that it was daytime. And as a group of giggling children ran around her, tugging at her dress and spinning her around in a circle, a wave of laughter washed over her. It was as if their innocence and playfulness had consumed her and for a moment she forgot her pain, threw her head back and laughed hysterically. When she opened her eyes she realized she was standing in front of the medieval knights again. The hair on the back of her neck bristled when she thought of it. Riding into battle with the knights, watching their shiny armor capture the sun as their lances clashed like thunder. It would be a marvelous thing to behold.

Shaking her head, she turned away. The time spent with the pirates had taught her a lot about herself, about how strong she really was and how determined she was to live so that she could fulfill her dream of finding a loving home to call her own. But there were many times she had faced death on her journey and she was not so sure she wanted to jump in to something so obviously dangerous, so quickly.

"They're something to look at, aren't they?" The husky voice from behind startled her. She felt someone walk up beside her and stop, resting, staring up at them with her.

"Yeah, but they're kinda scary."

"Many things in life are. Especially if you haven't experienced them before and don't know what to expect. But I gather," he said, rubbing the white stubble on his chin, "that you are the kind of young lady that doesn't shy away from adventure."

"Maybe…."

"No maybe's about it," he said quickly, shouldering the all too familiar mop as he began to walk away, "fear will keep you stuck right where you are. Do you like where you are Miss Jamie?"

His words struck a chord with her, appealing to her desire to be free of the orphanage and the evil Miss Legree who ran it. If she continued to avoid another adventure she may never figure a way out. And the thought of that old woman's wrinkly face all scrunched up like a sour prune as she swatted the air around her head with that horrible metal ruler, trying desperately to find a soft knuckle or the back of a calf to strike. *No! That's not going to be me! I'm never going back there again! Never!*

Clenching her fists tight she marched like a soldier, away from the dazzling knights and towards the punch bowl. Tonight would be the night. She was going to confront those men in shiny armor and make them take her with them. And as she sipped the punch, warm from sunlight, her head began to swim with ideas. Reaching over, she grabbed a piece of stiff cake, over sweetened with inexpensive icing. If she was going to be battling knights she would need her strength. So far, Jimbo had managed to leave behind a sandwich or two during the day for her to munch on. Some were resting next to the displays out in the open; others were left in the backroom, near the attic door. The odd thing is, she never actually saw him put the food down. She would turn her head one minute and then poof! There it was.

He knew her secret. And she knew his. And as the women in long, flowing dresses and matching flower hats tried to coral their over active children who were spinning like tops from all the sugar they had just ingested, she relaxed, knowing what she must do. And as she stepped outside the museum and sat on the steps, letting the wind flow through her chestnut hair and the sun warm her tear streaked face she closed her eyes and took it all in. The laughter of the young ones, the scolding of the exhausted mothers, the chirping of the birds that nestled in the nearby trees and the familiar swoosh, swoosh sound of the mop as old Jimbo cleaned the entrance behind her and finally the steps on which she sat.

# **Chapter 2**

Alone she waited in the janitor's room, peering out from behind the heavy curtains. The darkness of her dress would blend with the drapes but her lily white skin stood out in stark contrast. Night had come to the museum and with it all the dangers of being discovered. There was no crowd to blend in with now—just her and the night watchman.

It still made her chuckle the way he stomped around, wheezing like a dying animal, trying in vain to keep up with the beads of sweat that trickled down his rotund face, nestling themselves between his chins. He must have removed that soggy hanky from his pocket a dozen times and ran it across his furrowed brow. Finally, able to take it no longer, he sat on a thin folding chair in the lobby and leaned over, panting from exhaustion.

For a moment she felt sorry for him. Seeing someone struggle like that was never easy. It reminded her of the time a young girl of considerable weight had come to stay at the orphanage. She was nervous to be sure. And as she was ushered in to the school room with a stern hand pressed solidly against her lower back, everyone got quiet. They all stared at her, this new anomaly, dressed in a tattered pink dress with dirty, torn lace at the collar. Her filthy blond hair hung limply around her moon shaped face, tangled around a frayed headband.

Her name was **Sally**. And as she stood there in front of the firing squad, eyes downcast, gripping an old doll with curly red hair and a matching pink dress, letting the high, cackling voice of the old witch woman wash over her, a single tear trickled down her chubby cheek, staining the front of her dress. Jamie was the only one who noticed as the other girls were too busy whispering behind their hands and giggling at this pathetic creature before them.

She had been dropped off a week earlier at a different home, with only a hastily scribbled note pinned to her collar. They couldn't afford to take care of her anymore. She was an embarrassment to them, being so fat and unattractive. How could they be seen with her? Who would hire them with such a greedy looking child hanging around? It showed lack of discipline not only for her, but the parents as well. And the time was right. They were headed off to America in hopes of finding work. The land of opportunity they said; but only if you look the part.

Unfortunately the home where she was discarded was an all boy's establishment. Guess they didn't take the time to read the fine print on the sign when they shoved her out of the moving car that cold winter's morning. Too busy. And now she was here with them. If only there was a happy ending to this story. Jamie saw it coming a mile away. Being abused as much as she had, she learned to read the look in someone's eyes before they reacted to her. And when Sally made her way to her seat, a long, slender leg just happened to be sticking out in the aisle to trip her.

Down she went, face first on the hard floor. Her nose broke instantly and a loud *crunch* followed by streams of blood gushing down her face set the class into a proper frenzy. Before Miss Legree knew what happened the girls piled on top of her like a group of rowdy school boys playing football. They launched a full scale attack, pulling at her loose hair and slapping the back of her head. Thick, sausage arms trembled as she attempted to get up, only to crumble under their massive combined weight. And when Miss Legree had finally made her way over, the girls pretended as if they were helping her up.

"She fell," shouted one girl, patting Sally's arm as she feigned sympathy.

"It's really slippery you know," chimed in another.

"Be careful!"

"Let's ALL help her up together!"

Miss Legree nodded in approval. "That's the way girls! We all help each other to feel welcome!"

And as soon as she turned her back and walked over to the blackboard with a swirling of black skirts, they leaned over and pinched the new girl, hard. Digging in their long, glistening nails they spent so much time to manicure in hopes of being adopted, twisting her skin and pulling on it until it came out under their fingernails. Blood trickled down her arm, dripping from the ends of her fingertips, staining the floor. Jamie was in shock. She had experienced her share of bullying and mistreatment but never had she seen them come to together and act so aggressively. All she could do was watch as the frightened girl continued her slow, shuffling walk to the back, her doll still in hand.

That night, she disappeared from the orphanage. No fliers were sent out and no authorities were notified. She was just a girl—an orphan girl at that. No one could be bothered. A week later they found her body, frozen stiff to the ground in a dark alleyway. Her dress had been ripped down the front and there was dried blood on the insides of her thighs. There were no stab wounds, or signs of being strangled. She must have just given up and died right there in that alley. Jamie never quite got over that. It could have been her blood soaked and forgotten and she knew this.

But he was on the move again and now her options for escape were all but eliminated. Silently she cursed herself for reminiscing instead of planning her route to the mounted knights. With great guttural spasms he shuffled past the janitor's cloaked room and circled back around to the dinosaur display. There wasn't a moment to lose. Quick as a wink Jamie ran from the protective cave that housed her sleeping quarters and dove behind the Native American display just as he entered the room.

The tassels tickled her nose as did the dust from their unwashed dresses. Rearing her head back, she fought vainly to fight off a tremendous sneeze that worked its way from the pit of her stomach to the back of her eyeballs. Suddenly a loud *ping* sound followed by an angry barrage of muddled words filled the room. The buttons on his tight, white shirt had finally given way and were now flying around the room at lightning speed. One flew right by her ear, knocking over the crouching Indian man in the corner. Another flew into the janitor's room, nearly taking the curtains with it.

Her heart in her throat she watched as he decided which direction to go first. His eyes lingered for a moment on the Indian display, but as more buttons began to dislodge themselves he thought better of it and began to walk towards the black drapes that were now hanging slightly askew from the incident.

"Bartholomew," he muttered to himself as he strained to lean over and collect one of his fallen shirt guardians, "time to buy a larger size!"

Choking back laughter Jamie made a break for it—around the Indian display, down the hallway and past the dinosaur display. And finally, there they stood. In all their glory, those magnificent knights with sparkling armor and colored plumes bursting out of their helmets. Each held different colors. One donned green regalia and the other red. Their shields looked large and cumbersome in odd, upside down triangle shapes. And she couldn't imagine wearing what looked like a body suit made out of tin cans all day. Too hot!

A loud snoring sound from the back room let her know it was safe as she continued to stare up at them. "Guess he finally gave up," she said, listening to her voice echo.

The cardboard castle guarded by the knights looked truly pathetic. It had rippled and bent over at each corner after years of wear and the entrance was spray painted black to simulate an open gate. Only the person who did it wasn't very careful and got some of it on the gray parts of the castle. And as she continued to study the misshapen stones drawn with a trembling hand, the floor underneath her began to rumble. At first she thought it was nothing and dismissed it due to lack of sleep.

But then it happened again, only this time it was much louder than before. Quickly her eyes darted around the room, looking for any sign of unrest. Nothing seemed to be out of place. The dinosaurs stood, some flying, some perched on the edge of the ceiling, open mouthed and ready to gobble up the first unlucky person who walked on by. The knights hadn't moved either. They sat rigid atop their starched white stallions, lances posed; ready for a battle that was never to be.

Several minutes passed. Now she was getting uneasy. *How was she supposed to go on an adventure if they didn't come to life?* Tapping her foot impatiently she huffed out loud waving her finger at mounted men in metal.

"Well? What's taking you so long?" Silence.

"What does a girl have to do to get some attention? Do you HEAR me?!?" Nothing. Now she was really getting upset.

"You useless idiots," She bellowed, "What's the point of all this anyway? Wish Jimbo was here, I'd give HIM a piece of my mind—I would!"

As soon as the name "Jimbo" was uttered the rumbling returned in earnest. The walls began to shake and she watched in horror as the dinosaur display, along with large sections of the ceiling, came crashing to the ground. *What had she done now? Was the museum going to swallow her whole?* Crouching down she covered her head in order to avoid being knocked unconscious as the sounds all around her began to blend together in some sort of mismatched harmony.

Closing her eyes tight her other senses came alive as a distinct, click—clack, click—clack, of what sounded like an army of women in high heels trampled across the floor. Curiosity getting the better of her, she cracked open her left eye, just enough to see the thin, blurry version of what was going on. A sea of hairy, white legs and brilliant boots blew past, coming to rest on the opposite side of her body before they vanished down the hallway.

For a moment she sat, frozen with fear. *Was she dead?* But as the familiar noises echoed in her ears she realized life was still with her. Keeping her arms in front of her face, she stood up slowly, taking a long, hard look around. The museum was in shambles with large, swaying pieces of the marble dangling from the ceiling and dinosaur bones scattered all around. The floor was covered in a fine, white powder that looked something akin to sugar, surrounding the broken marble squares.

Timidly, she walked down the corridor towards the dinosaur display, hoping against hope that something was still standing. The hallway was dark and eerie as the faint security lights cast oddly shaped shadows all around. As Jamie reached the end of the hall, a terrific sound of crashing thunder could be heard, growing more intense by the minute. *Had the dinosaurs come to life?* Clutching her hand to her chest, she pushed forward; praying whatever it was did not like the taste of little girls.

Standing at the entrance to the dinosaur exhibit, her heart sank. Every skeleton, including the big tyrannosaurus rex in the center of the room, was broken into a million pieces. Fragments of bone covered the floor, from the front double doors to the red, glowing exit sign in the back. For a moment she felt a hot surge of anger sweep over her, starting in her toes and moving to the hairs on her scalp.

True, the dinosaurs were big and scary and yes, they always made her feel that she was going to be eaten at any given moment. But, they were *hers.* Somehow, during her stay, she had grown attached to these skeletal monsters. And every time she walked past them she knew exactly where she was in the museum. Never mind their razor sharp teeth, or their claws that looked as though they could easily tear you in two. They had become a source of comfort—of familiarity. Like the North Star for sailors.

And as she stood, contemplating her loss, an earsplitting clang distracted her attention. From down the opposite hall they came running at full speed. The one in red adornments was the first to attack, crouching low in the saddle and positioning his lance at his opponent's gut. His white steed blew hot steam from his nostrils and pawed the floor in anticipation. The heavy armor glittered under the minimal lights as he circled the dinosaur bones, poised for battle.

"Are ye ready, lord Crewe? Have thou given thoughts to who will lay claim to your lands, your wife and your children once I have administered your proper thrashing?"

His long helmet that reached his chest hid any facial expressions, but Jamie could guess there was an ugly sneer hidden behind that metal protector.

"Lord Destrian, let us not waste time with idle threats. Rather, let our lances sing our praises as we connect as warriors on the battle field!"

His words were strong and calm, this knight in green, and as they bounced around the main entrance Jamie decided it would be him that she would pursue for this adventure. But the hour was growing late and as she watched the men prance, gallop and then collide, catapulting shards of ceiling remnants and broken bones around the room, she began to grow desperate. Soon, it would be daylight and the rays of the golden sun would wash over the museum, turning the knights back to statues and taking with them all hope of embarking on the next adventure.

"You only get one chance miss," he told her one lazy afternoon as the bugs hummed nosily in the thick heat.

"One chance for what?" They were sitting on entrance steps, sipping cool lemonade that Jimbo had packed for his lunch. It would be cooler that night, she guessed, taking a long, slow slurp from her glass.

"They are fickle creatures and only give a person a single opportunity to grab hold. If you miss it, all may be lost."

And with that he crumpled up his brown paper bag and tossed it into the metal bin on the side of the building. Then, humming a tuneless hymn, he gathered his mop and bucket, which were never very far away and disappeared through the lobby doors. This gave her much to think about and provided great motivation as she considered her next move. They only had eyes for each other as they connected with such intensity, tearing deep gashes into the metal body suits and loose hanging chain mail.

Soft, orange rays began to sneak in through the glass doors, sending shockwaves of panic through her body. Swallowing her fear of being trampled under those mighty hooves, she dashed into the center of the room, where the tyrannosaurus rex had once stood and raised her hands high above her head. At that moment, one of the sunbeams touched the back of the horse's leg, causing it to stiffen. It was happening—they were turning back into statues!

"Hey!" she shouted, flailing her arms like a drowning woman, "hey, hey, hey!"

They did not see her, or if they did, they were too intent on destroying each other to pay much attention. There was nothing else she could do. Taking a deep breath, she did the most frightening thing she could think of. Bending her knees until her backside almost touched the floor, she jumped head first in front of one of the horses. She felt something hard and warm hit her shoulder as she tumbled to the ground; and then the painful smack of her back connecting with the floor.

Jamie lay in a heap, moaning with pain. Her arms and legs were like wet noodles, lying limply beside her body. She had hit her head and began to babble as the room turned dark, swallowing her whole. The next thing she knew she was being carried in strong arms, hovering above the marble floor like an angel. Angry voices echoed all around her as she faded in and out of consciousness. A few minutes later she awoke, sitting atop a hard, leather saddle in the middle of the museum.

It seemed she had fallen in to the red knight's horse, causing it to rear, pitching him off the saddle and on to his backside. The knight in green was arguing for her safe keeping, saying it would be better if she went with him. His voice was pleading but firm.

"This young lady needs proper care. Her wounds could be far greater than can be seen."

"Then let her come with me, so that after she is cared for her debt can be repaid. It is I who was injured here and so the decision lies with me!"

Reluctantly the green knight agreed, stepping aside as the man in red marched up to his horse and yanked her to the ground. Without a word he flung her on top of his horse and then jumped up behind. She felt the stiff armor dig into her back as he leaned forward, urging his horse onward.

"Hold tightly m'lady," urged a gentle voice from beside them, "or you will surely fall once more."

She could not respond as her head wobbled from side to side like a rag doll. Her thighs began to ache and sweat as she slid alarmingly, unable to stop herself. Then suddenly, gentle hands reached over and grabbed her, interlacing her fingers with the horse's mane.

"Keep your hands on your own horse," yelled the man in red, "this wench is my property now!"

And with that, he brought the horse to a gallop, heading straight for the cardboard castle as the sun filled the room. Jamie's head began to spin as they jumped over the display bar, hitting the flimsy wood patch of floor just in front of the castle. *Where were they going?* And as they charged at full speed straight for the dark mouth that was the drawbridge, a voiceless scream that turned into a gurgle escaped her throat. *They were going to run straight through the display and into the wall!*

# **Chapter 3**

With a mighty *thud* they landed and continued to gallop at full speed. Jamie's eyes were shut so tight tears began to trickle out, leaving salty streaks on her flushed cheeks. It took her a moment to realize that she was still alive as the sound of the pounding hooves meeting with the earth filled her ears. Ducking behind her forearm she opened her eyes just enough to see the blades of green grass come flying at her, mixed with dirt and small rocks as the stallion's feet dug deep into the soft earth, churning it up like bowl of lumpy stew.

Turning her head she wiped her face on the animal's mane, smearing the dirt and sweat across her brow. Strands of wiry hair tickled her face, causing her to sit straight up in the saddle and face her new environment. The insides of her thighs burned as she bounced around, feeling the stiff leather rub against her soft flesh each time she came down on the saddle.

"Ouch, ouch, ouch!" she yelled, trying to tuck her brown dress in between her legs and the unforgiving leather.

But with her legs spread so far apart, her dress had to be pulled up past her hips in order to accommodate the straightness of the garment. In books she had seen women with long, flowing gowns that nearly covered the entire body of the horse, riding peacefully through a secluded meadow filled with wild flowers. Their faces were calm and serene as they stared off into the distance with a dreamy expression in their eyes. Oh, how deceived she had been!

Lifting her head up she tried to look around and get her bearings but nothing looked familiar. They were tearing through an open field with no flowers or trees in sight. Brownish green mud covered the ground indicating a previously heavy rain and the cloudless sky housed a relentless, burning sun that scorched the back of her unprotected neck.

She tried to keep her eyes open, searching in vain for the green knight--her savior in a sea of hopelessness. But they were alone, the two of them, holding on for dear life to a wild—eyed animal who had just moments ago reared so violently it had thrown its rider, someone familiar, to the ground. She shuddered to think of what it would do to her. And as the wind whipped across her face, stinging her eyes, she bowed her head once again and prayed for a miracle.

"Alright then, dismount!"

They had stopped moving and were now standing next to a run—down stable that was attached to a great, stone wall. Jamie shook her head in disbelief, unable to tell if they were still moving or not.

"Come on then wench! I'll not be carting you around like some noblewoman to be sure!"

With her vision swirling in front of her, she slid from the saddle, landing hard on her backside. Luckily, a pile of nearby hay broke her fall, wrapping its crunchy arms around her in an awkward embrace. Tilting her head back her eyes followed the massive stone wall until it broke apart into columns that sprouted what looked like large crowns near the top. Small windows covered in brightly colored stain glass covered the columns, each containing a different picture of a Biblical story, illuminated by the harsh sun light.

Mary and Joseph glowed as they hovered over a baby Jesus in a manger, their large, round halos encompassing the space behind their heads like yellow moons. The baby was nearly naked, covered only by a strip of swirling cloth that lay between His genitals and over His shoulder. No one was smiling but a faraway look of holiness gave their faces a sort angelic demeanor as Mary and Joseph stared down adoringly at their child who was looking up and to the left with His little chubby arms spread wide open as a gesture of acceptance.

Maybe it was the stress of all that had happened, but for some reason Jamie found the scene so moving tears sprang to her eyes gray eyes, making them turn cloudy like a sky after a rough storm.

"Get up wench," bellowed an all too familiar voice, "and tend to your duties!"

He had already led the horse under the awning of the stable and tied it to a wooden bar. The heavy helmet was tucked under his right arm revealing a face as ugly as his personality. Deep puncture wounds covered his cheeks, making him look like a piece of Swiss cheese. Stringy black hair hung in his eyes and down the back of his neck, the ends dripping with sweat like icicles melting from a rooftop. Thin, colorless lips and a long, hooked nose completed the look as he stood, stomping his armored leg, red faced with impatience.

Never had she seen a man so grotesque looking. Some of the pirates from her previous adventure had been strange looking to be sure. Her mind returned to the tall man with the lumpy face with two chins and long, bony fingers. He made a stand in her defense when she tried to get something to eat with the rest of the pirates after scrubbing the deck all day in the hot sun. But there was something more sinister about this knight's appearance. It was as if his evil personality was too much to contain in bodily form and had burned its way through his skin for the outside world to see.

Jamie considered it a warning but unfortunately this warning came too late and now she was stuck with this arrogant, angry man who was demanding something of her of which she had no knowledge.

"You stand and gaze about like a common poop-noddy![1] Clean my armor and rub down my horse!"

She stared at him, uncertain of what to do first. Slowly, she moved towards the horse that was covered with a thick layer of salt from the hard ride. With a quick glance she realized the sweat had pooled under the saddle and so she grabbed the leather seat and tried to pull it off in order to clean the animal properly. It didn't budge.

"That's strange," she mumbled as she walked around the horse, studying it from all angles.

Never having been around such an animal, she had no idea how to remove a saddle and so she tried again with as much gusto as she could muster, grunting and screaming aloud in frustration. This time it moved. Unfortunately it moved under the horse, sliding along the wetness of the animal's back. She let go as it flipped upside down, falling back on the wooden floor. From this angle she could see that there were straps that hooked together, keeping the saddle in place. But the knight was in no mood for a lengthy learning experience.

"Little wallydraigle![2] Of what good are you to anyone?" Turning his head he hollered into the shadowy barn, "boy!" so loud the rafters shook. A low rustling sound followed by a cloud of dust and hoof clippings rolled out the open doorway and settled at his shiny feet.

---

[1] *simpleton*

[2] *useless woman*

He had short brown hair that grazed the top of his earlobes and tickled his long eyelashes. A white shirt with puffy sleeves, stained brown from years of hard labor hung low over a pair of thin tights. The shirt was much too large for him, forcing him to improvise a piece of frayed cord for a belt. His feet would have been bare, except someone had given him a pair of shoes to wear, only that someone had much larger feet and so pieces of old leather had been wrapped around his ankles, anchoring them to his legs. Streaks of dirt ran up and down his young forehead and his fingernails were caked with black dirt.

"Yes m'lord?" Green eyes sparkled under heavy lashes as he stood stock still, await his instructions.

"Clean my armor and this beast! And teach her the proper way! She is to be my new theow[3]. Train her well or my whip shall leave its mark across your back!"

"As you wish m'lord."

And with that the red knight stomped away, leaving the two of them alone in the noon day heat. She studied his face as he moved around, graceful as a cat. They would be the same age, she decided, or something close to it. At first he didn't look at her. He made himself busy gathering buckets of water and hard bristle brushes. Neat and quick, that was his style, not even spilling a drop of water as the horse backed in to him, knocking the bucket in his hand. With an exasperated sigh he dipped the brush into the bucket and then began scrubbing the horse.

"You should mind the back," he said, leaning down to dip his scrubber in the now soapy water, "it is where they hold the sweat from the saddle."

Jamie nodded following his every movement as they worked side by side in the shade. Sweat ran down her back, soaking her underwear as she pushed the brush around in small circles, taking care to flick it up at the end. Their breathing took on a rhythm of its own as the sun climbed up further into the blue sky chasing away what little shade the awning provided. Her arms and shoulders ached as the hour wore on, draining her spirit with each drop of thick sweat that fell from her brow, soaking the earth.

"How—how much longer?"

___

[3] slave

He didn't respond at first. The only sound she heard was the whisk, whisk of the brush as he finished the haunches around the tail. Without a word he put down his brush and walked over to the other side of the horse. The only things visible were his legs and as she let her scrubber fall to the ground the scene before her went blurry as her mind began to wander back to the musty little classroom at the orphanage.

"Ladies! Sit up straight please! We have someone special coming in to speak with us today!" Miss Legree looked so proud of herself she was positively bursting.

It wasn't unusual to have a guest speaker in their tiny classroom. Everyone was interested in doing charity work. It made them sound good to all their friends and family even if they were horrible beasts. And a girl's orphanage with limited funds was considered a double minority. So needless to say it was the hotbed of activity for the wealthy businessmen who grew bored from living in luxury and decided to spend a day in the life of the poor and unfortunate as they were called.

"Mr. Benson! Mr. Benson!" Miss Legree waved furiously from the front of the classroom, signaling it was okay for him to proceed forward and join her.

In sauntered a sharply dressed gentleman in a heavy wool coat and matching stovepipe hat. A thick, black mustache covered his upper lip as he moved slowly between the crowded desks, tapping his walking stick along the way. His cane was something of great interest to Jamie. The wood was stained dark and worn smooth, covered in a shiny coat of sealer. At the head was a white knob with pink and purple flowers painted in a delicate circle. She had never seen anything like it and the longer she stared the more the click, click, click sound along with the shimmering wood seemed to hypnotize her. And as he passed by she just couldn't resist reaching out to touch it.

An incredible *whack* sent her reeling back, knocking the wind out of her as the stick came flying across her desk. The pain was exquisite as the hard wood smacked solidly against her chest and shoulders. Jamie's first instinct was to cover her face as she ducked down on the ground beside her desk. Her heart was racing as she kept her head tucked into her knees and her arms over her head. The steady creaking sound of his footsteps moving towards her made true panic settle in as she waited for the inevitable.

A pair of expensive brown shoes with stiffly tied laces stopped in front of her crouched form. She waited, not daring to move or scarcely breathe. The room was deathly quiet as all eyes focused on her. She could feel their cold, judgmental gaze penetrating her back as they waited with her. The man's shoes had little bumps on the side where the laces protruded. And the toes were shined within an inch of their lives. Dark pant legs covered the socks, but Jamie imagined they would be thickly knitted to keep his feet warm on cold winter days.

Suddenly she realized she could not see the tip of his cane touching the floor. But it was too late. The heavy stick had made its way across her exposed back, cracking against her spine. A gasp that turned into a scream shot out of her, as she fell forward, rolling into the fetal position in the corner. The room buzzed with excitement.

"What is the meaning of this?" The headmistress had come out from behind her desk to see what was going on. She stopped in between Jamie and Mr. Benson looking back and forth, waiting for an answer.

"No problem here," the man said calmly, placing the tip of his walking stick back on the floor, "just teaching the young one a lesson about the meaning of private property." He nodded towards Jamie as he spoke.

After a moment of awkward silence the headmistress in black cleared her throat and said, "Well now that that's settled." And led him back to the front of the class. Jamie was left to writhe in pain on the floor while the other girls bowed their heads, laughing uncontrollably.

The next thing she heard was Miss Legree say: "And now class, I would like to introduce you to Mr. John Benson. He owns several horse farms here in England and has been gracious enough to take some time out of his busy schedule to come visit with us. Mr. Benson."

He took the front of the room, standing proud as you please in the center so that everyone could get a good look at him. A flurry of hands went up to ask questions before he even began.

"How many different horses are there?"

"Do you get to ride them all the time?"

"Can we go see your farms?"

Miss Legree looked flustered as she tried to get the girls to control themselves. "Let the man speak first." Her face was bright red.

"Oh, don't worry about it," he said lightly, patting her on the arm, "they're just a bunch of curious youngsters is all."

After that Jamie stopped listening. She spent the remainder of the class sitting in the corner, facing the wall, waiting for the pain to go away. So whatever information he had offered about horses, she missed.

A bucket of cool water splashed across her face washed away her day dreams as the stable boy threw it over the back of the horse, making a direct hit. She yelled with surprise, enjoying the wetness on her warm skin, feeling it drip down her chest and stomach. He stood on tip toe and peeked over the back of the horse.

"Sorry about that!"

He didn't look like he was sorry. In fact he had the beginnings of a smile on his dimpled cheeks as he worked around her, whistling loudly. Pieces of old, dry cloth were brought out next as the two of them worked feverishly to dry the large animal. The sun dipped low in the sky by the time a messenger delivered the knight's armor to be cleaned and shined. Jamie yawned loudly, taking a moment to rest herself on the same pile of hay that had first broken her fall.

"You take rest now. I'll clean the armor." She stared at him in amazement.

"But then how will I learn....."

"I will show you later. Go to bed. Lord Destrian will have you up before the sun."

And with that he ushered her in to the barn. A lone candle was their only source of light as they maneuvered their way around large pieces of equipment that cluttered the floor and suits of armor that hung from the walls on large hooks. They looked like they could take on a life of their own and she shuddered to think of them walking around without anyone inside as they banged noisily against the walls in the wind. Just around the corner was a rundown shack made from sticks, mud and old bricks. It was built on a slant, the roof sliding dangerously towards the ground and the front door swinging open like a dark, gaping mouth.

She stumbled inside and sat at a low, wooden bench as he hurriedly prepared a small fire. There wasn't much in there. Just a small wooden chair, a bench that was used as a table, the fireplace and a lumpy mattress in the corner. But somehow the warm glow of the fire seemed to make everything better and she found herself drawn to it, warming her hands as the boy prepared a small bed of hay in the other corner.

"Will this suit you m'lady?" She smiled as he gestured towards the pile of clean hay. Without another word she lay on a thin blanket as he tucked another one around her body.

"This will keep you warm. This cruck[4] is small enough so the fire will keep you comfortable all night."

She tried to nod in response but found that her head was too heavy. And by the time he made it to the door she was already asleep; surrendering herself to a deep and peaceful slumber.

---

[4] *peasant house*

# Chapter 4

The morning came on quickly and as Jamie lay in a snug straw bed with a roaring fire to warm her bones the sounds of the **cruck** took on their own melody. First there was the wind that whistled through the holes in the walls, wailing like an old man with an aching back. Then, the crooked door that rattled on its rusty hinges like a rambunctious child shaking a new toy. Soft droplets of morning dew plopped heavily into cracked pots set under the many holes in the roof. In truth, the room looked like a pottery market with an untold number of chipped, faded bowls scattered across the floor. And every once in awhile the crackling fire would *hiss* softly as a fat teardrop fell into the mixture of red, yellow and blue flames, tucked neatly under a crumbling chimney.

A robin with a belly bluer than the deepest ocean perched itself on a branch just outside one of the tiny windows. His black eyes sparkled as he cocked his tiny head to one side before opening his small, pointed beak and letting out a melody so sweet it would make the angels weep. It reminded her of a mother singing her child to sleep, while cradling her gently in her arms. She was so taken with the peacefulness of the moment the angry footsteps that turned up gravel and grit alike were not noticed until it was too late.

With a hideous *wham* the door to the run down house was thrown open, nearly taking it off its hinges at it crashed into the wall behind it. And before she knew what was happening the warm blanket was ripped off her trembling form, exposing her to the elements. He stood between them, these two sleeping servants, hot with rage.

"Up now you sloomy[5] theows! Mind my horse and armor before I suggill[6] you about the legs and backside!"

Every vein in his neck was bulging as he spoke, surrounding his Adam's apple like long, purple snakes. Broken blood vessels turned crimson around his hooked nose as his enormous fists began to pound the ground where she slept. Never had she shot out of bed so quickly, wrapping her arms around her chest for warmth as she backed away, towards the fire. Her knees

---

[5] *lazy/sleepy*
[6] *beat*

trembled as her eyes struggled for focus. The morning mist had found its way into the cabin making it all seem like a bad dream.

"At once Lord Destrian! Forgive our dringle.[7] I shall be with you at once!"

He always seemed to know what to say, that stable boy with the mysterious emerald eyes. And as Jamie watched him hop about like a rabbit with a fire poker attached to his tail, a twinge of familiarity tickled her gut. There was something about him, about the way he moved and spoke that reminded her of someone. But it was too early in the morning for brain racking and so she tucked that thought away for a later time; gulping down a glass of lukewarm milk he had poured for her before dashing out into the cool morning mist.

Four hours later when her arms and back ached worse than they ever had before, it was time for a break. A lunch of "maw-wallop[8] that would fill the empty spot in their bellies and not much else" as the stable boy put it, was served cold, wrapped in a large, dirty cloth that was thrown on the barn floor in front of them. Never had her stomach rumbled so loudly, not even when she was held for days without food in the bottom of the pirate ship had her hunger been so ravenous. With an enthusiastic *swish* she flung open the ratted cloth, praying for meat and fresh vegetables, or maybe even a fruit of some sort. But what she saw made her stomach turn.

Three large strips of dried, wrinkled meat lay in the center of the deeply stained fabric. Surrounding it was a thin, red liquid that had obviously leaked from somewhere, accompanied by tiny seeds and random globs of pulp. The sight made her recoil and the smell was even worse. She couldn't be sure if it was from the dirty blanket with its various dried puddles, or the fact that whatever it was they were being served had been left to rot in the sun for an undisclosed amount of time. All she knew was that her morning milk was climbing its way up from her belly to her throat, making her heave uncontrollably.

Turning her head, she back away from the blanket just as the stable boy swooped in to rescue the situation. With a wave of his hand the cloth was overturned and tucked neatly away, while the food was spread lovingly on a clean hay bale set directly in the middle of the floor. It was like a little table and as they sat on either side, Jamie staring at what appeared to food with a

---

[7] *lazy manner*
[8] *badly cooked food*

mixture of disgust and curiosity, and him whisking around the various contents of the care package, dividing it up evenly between them. The dried brown strips were meat, he explained, and yes they were supposed to look and taste like that. It was a way in which soldiers could keep food in their bags for weeks without it spoiling.

The red liquid, as it turned out, came from a pair of soft tomatoes that had been tossed carelessly in the bag at the last minute, being brutally mashed along the long and bumpy ride. It didn't matter though. The salty, stiff meat took a long time for her to lick and soften enough to break apart and put in her mouth. It was the chewiest thing Jamie had ever eaten. And before she knew it, it was time to go back to work again.

Sweeping out the stalls and grooming the horses was hard work. And she was certain she had never seen an animal poop as much as these ones did. The hay bales were quite heavy and so it was up to the stable boy to stack them neatly in the overhead loft, while Jamie rigged them up with a rope and pulley to help get them there. At first she felt awkward and out of place, as if she was hindering his rhythm more than helping. But by the end of the day she felt she had the hang of it and for once she felt like an asset to the situation.

And then she saw it, tall and glittering at the front of the barn, catching the last rays of daylight in its metallic flesh. He had returned on horseback, the knight in red, bringing with him another hours worth of scrubbing and polishing. The horse was dark with sweat, frothing at the mouth as the impatient rider worked the bit, making him trot back and forth in the unforgiving heat.

"Come now you mumpers![9] Must I wait about all day while you drift in and out of consciousness, spending your time under the shade of the steadfast barn which my earnings have built?"

With a shuffling of unsteady feet the stable boy appeared, sweat glistening on his brow. Crouching down low, he bowed humbly before his master casting his eyes to the floor. A loud clinking sound followed by jingling footsteps as the knight descended from his horse and approached the servile youth filled the quiet evening air.

---

[9] *beggars*

"Take them boy," he sneered, smacking the leather reigns angrily across his bare back.

Jamie watched for any sign of discontent, studying the crouched frame at the knight's feet. If he felt pain or fear he did not show it. Nimble finger interlaced with the reigns dangling in front of his young face and with eyes still cast downwards he quickly guided the horse to the holding post just outside the barn for a rub down. She followed close behind not wishing to endure what was left of the red rider's animosity.

"You clean the horse while I tend to our lord," whispered the level minded youth.

Jamie nodded to show that she understood; unbuckling the heavy saddle and placing it on the post to air dry as she gathered the buckets and brushes to begin the job. Her hands were trembling as she dipped them into the lukewarm water. All day she had worked and even though the barn offered protection from the sun, the ungodly heat had gotten to her. Black spots flashed in front of her eyes as she wavered in front of the exhausted animal. Grabbing onto its long, flowing mane she steadied herself, taking in deep breaths of air through her nose and mouth.

Meanwhile the stable boy was busy undressing the knight from his armor and placing it tenderly to the side to be cleaned. He moved methodically around the massive frame, starting with his helmet so that he could breathe easier and then working his way down. To make up for the height difference, he used hay bales as step stools, taking great care to properly unhook each piece before moving on to the next.

She was impressed by how fast and clean he worked, never missing a beat even when the knight grew irritable and began to wave his arms in protest. It would have to be learned, this method of removing the armor. Not that she wanted to be that close to a man who could fly off the handle at a moment's notice; but if the boy fell ill or if she could repay him in any way for all the nice things he had done for her so far, this might be it.

Before she knew it they were both finished. Maybe she had cut a few corners, not pushing the brush as deep as she could have into the horse's coat and skipping the mane all together. She knew he would notice. How could he not. That animal was his livelihood and as he sauntered over to inspect her work, the hands which trembled from exhaustion began to tingle with newfound strength as the previously discarded brush found its way back to the horse and the neglected mane.

Another hour passed before she was certain her work would pass even the most detailed of inspections and with a mighty heave she threw the brush down on the ground and kicked over the bucket of sudsy water. The sun had already buried itself behind the horizon, giving way to a tiny sliver of a moon, standing alone in a black, starless sky. At least the heat had subsided and as the cool night air found her sweaty back, shivers crawled up and down her bony spine.

"Come now," said a gentle voice behind her, "it is time to go inside and sit by the warm fire."

Without a word she obeyed, stumbling towards the sad little shack as he led the now spotless animal into his stall. Thick chunks of mud stuck to her shoes, sucking them down to the ground like a thirsty child slurping a soda. An aggravated scream escaped her throat as she reached down and pulled her shoes from the mud pit.

"How is it there is always mud when it doesn't seem to rain?" She wondered aloud.

"The grass doesn't grow here anymore. And it gets muddy because of all the water we throw out after cleaning the horses, m'lady."

Jamie smiled sheepishly. She should have figured that one out on her own. The **cruck** was downhill from the barn. Naturally the buckets of water would have to go somewhere. They walked side-by-side, drinking in the cool night air, letting it envelope their wet bodies. Once inside the hut Jamie stood by the fire to get warm, inspecting her brown dress. It had been through a lot already; first the pirate ship and now this. A small hole had formed at the bottom near the hem and the front was smeared with black mud.

"You'll be needing some new clothes then, something right proper for a stable girl."

He smiled as he brushed past, throwing a warm piece of cloth her way. She rubbed it against her cheek, feeling the coarseness of the material mixed with the warmness and the smell of something fresh and clean. Soap! Oh how she longed to take a bath. But looking around the bare room she saw no tub or spigot for water to flow through. And then she saw him, naked as the day was long, standing in the corner hunched over a large bucket, washing himself.

"I'll be done in a minute. Then I'll get you some fresh water."

She stood there speechless, staring at his bare bottom. It was round and white like two large snowballs packed hard before a good fight. His body was lean without an ounce of fat to be seen and a weird sort of patch work tan. From the neck up he was brown as a berry, but his torso and legs were exquisitely pale. His arms from the elbow down were also dark standing in stark contrast to the shining, pearl like skin on the rest of him.

He bathed quickly, dunking his head in last before wrapping a small cloth around his waist and leaning out the window to toss out the dirty water. It was her turn next and as she stood before the pool of clear water dancing in the bottom of the ruddy bucket, her uneasiness became apparent. Clearing his throat, he scooped up two, long blankets and tacked them first to the wall and then to each other, held strong by a chair in the middle and a long wooden stick that had been tied to the arm.

With a grateful nod she dove behind the blanket fortress and began her cleansing. And while she scrubbed with borrowed soap, first her hair, then her torso and finally her toes, she began to think over the day's events. Hard work was not the problem. She had done without and worked hard her entire life, never expecting anything from anyone. But being forced into slave labor from dawn 'till dusk was not something she was prepared to take lying down. Even Miss Legree had insisted that girls should take a break every now and then.

"A young lady should be quiet and conservative, always supporting the views of her husband and her parents."

It was another dreadful Monday morning made even worse by the fact it pouring down rain outside, flooding the otherwise bustling playground. Usually, they would have what was known as quiet time, in which reading music, writing poetry, or practicing sewing was encouraged. But since they had very few books to read from, Jamie found it best to situate herself in the corner, close her eyes and day dream the hours away.

"There should be adequate time given to your husband, the children you will bear and," she added with her long, bony finger pointed straight up in the air, "yourself. That's right girls I want you to always make time for yourself."

"But what about cooking and cleaning and laundry and stuff," asked a wide—eyed brunet in the front row.

"Ah yes, it is true," the schoolmarm purred, sounding like a drowning cat, "all these task must be accomplished in order to be considered a proper wife and mother. But none-the-less, if only for a few moments a day, you should set aside some time in which to do whatever it is that makes you happy."

Jamie was stunned when she heard this. The only form of gospel that had been preached in the orphanage was hard work and subservience. Could it be that the winds of reason and change had finally blown in?

"Of course when I say whatever makes you happy I mean something productive for your family like sewing, learning to play the piano, or improving your dancing skills. These are all things that add to the desirability of a young lady."

Jamie snorted loudly. She might have known there would have been a catch. None of these things interested her. They were all so deadly dull and boring. Miss Legree heard her and made eye contact for the briefest of moments, her old brown eyes melting into her young soul as she glared menacingly in her direction. Crossing her arms, Jamie glared back, refusing to back down to the old witch in black. She was going to ask her if she had anything to say in front of the class, but then thought better of it. She had learned her lesson before, the hard way. Turning back to the blackboard she continued to drone on about stockings and petticoats while Jamie doodled on the top of her desk with a chewed up pencil, alone in the back of the room.

"You alright m'lady? You've been in there awhile."

"Ah? Oh!" She shook her head, remembering where she was.

Slowly she emerged from the protective cocoon of the blankets into the nippy air of the hole ridden shack. A small piece of coarse cloth was all that stood between her and the roving eyes of the stable boy who was doing his best to look away. A roaring fire drew her in, tempting her to linger and warm her icy toes.

"I set up the laundry line. You can hang your clothes on it when you're done," he added, pointing to the long, thin string that had been pegged above the fireplace.

The last thing she felt like doing was more cleaning, but as she stared down at her muddy dress, she knew the itchiness that would ensue if it was not properly cleaned. Reusing her bath water she made quick work of taking the big stains out of her ratted dress and underwear, hanging them over a sizzling fire, listening to it spit and hiss as the water from her damp clothing dripped down below.

"Do you know how to sew?"

She stared up at him, raising one eyebrow in question. No, she shook her head, she did not know how to sew. It was never necessary before. All their dresses from the orphanage were made by nuns who thrived on charity work. Knitting was an optional past time but never considered a necessity.

"Ah, just as well then. Seems a bit strange you know--a girl that doesn't know how to sew. No offense."

"None taken. It just wasn't something I had to do where I grew up."

He turned towards her, more curious than ever. "Where did you grow up?'

Jamie smiled, shaking her head at the thought of trying to explain it. "Somewhere very far away."

"Over the mountains you mean? Past the valley of unrest?"

"Something like that. Anyways let's start with something easier. Like a name?"

He hesitated for a moment, dropping his soapy shirt back into the bucket. He was still naked but somehow she had forgotten about that. There was something about this mysterious stranger that rang true.

"Aldwin. What's yours?"

"Aldwin? What kind of a name is that?"

She could have kicked herself as soon as she heard the words come tumbling out of her mouth. Perhaps he took it the wrong way. She glanced over, studying his face. But he was smiling back at her, ready to explain.

"It means *old friend*. I know, I know, it's a family name. What could I do?"

She smile and nodded. "My name is Jamie and I don't know what it means."

"And you thought my name was strange?" A smile broke across his face as he attempted to suppress his giggles.

"What's wrong with Jamie? It's better than Aldwin!" Now she was getting offended. *After all, who was he to tease her?*

"Maybe where you come from but not here. Look," he said in soothing tone, seeing that she was upset, "let's just say that we both come from different lands and leave it at that."

The anger broke from her, running out like a leaky pot. She was too tired to fight and after all he was the only friend she had.

"Can you teach me how to take off the knight's armor?"

"Sure, in the morning. But let's practice on a straw man first. Lord Destrian doesn't like to be practiced on if you know what I mean."

Boy, did she! "I know. Good night Aldwin," she said, snuggling her naked skin against the straw and rough blanket.

"Good night miss Jamie," he said before turning his back to sleep.

Alarm bells went off in her head but she was too tired to stay awake contemplating what it meant. It was the same term of affection used by Jimbo at the museum. *But it couldn't possibly be him.....could it*

# Chapter 5

In the days that followed she fell into a routine of cleaning out the stable and then the horses, making certain they were all fed and watered before heading off to bed. Aldwin tried to teach her how to remove the knight's armor, taking great pains to set up a straw filled dummy made of old gunny sacks and tied off with old bits of rope to give it that human feel. Alone in the barn after a scarce meal of rotten vegetables and jerky they would practice until her fingers grew sore from all the bucking and unbuckling of leather straps that held the metal garment in place. Then it was off to tend the returning horses the knight used to practice during the day.

"Why does he need so many different horses to ride? Can't he use just one?"

The sun was unusually low in the sky bringing down with it all the heat and pestilence of the swarming, biting mosquitoes. It began to rain nightly and the puddles of standing, stagnant water gave off a foul odor they seemed to be most attracted to. Red, swollen bumps covered her arms and legs making her itch uncontrollably. A low chucked emerged from her barnyard companion.

"No miss Jamie. You see, Lord Destrian is preparing for the yearly joust and the manner in which he rides wears the beasts out. They would die of the heat if he took just one."

She nodded her head as if she understood, wracking her brain in an attempt to remember what a joust was. The term had been used before when Miss Legree was prancing around in her long, black dress at the front of the classroom. It was another typical day in the orphanage with the room uncomfortably hot and the steam from their breath fogging up the windows. Air conditioning was only used on special occasions and with the funds for the girl's home being cut back a little more each year, the cost would be too much for them to bear. And so they suffered, cramped together like sardines in a tiny classroom with no ventilation.

"A knight," her shrill voice sang out, "is a man of dignity and honor, who roams about the countryside defending his king and his fellow noblemen."

Over in the corner, near the blackboard, a poster of a knight all decked out in his shiny armor had been pasted to the wall. It was old and ratty, probably on loan from the local library, or saved from a neighboring garbage bin. Long folds ran through the center of the picture, distorting the already fuzzy image. Small tears surrounded the border, hanging open and loose like dog's tongues panting in the heat. Whatever its original color was supposed to be would forever remain a mystery as brown aged stains covered the flimsy surface.

"So….a knight is a good guy?" She always had to ask the questions, sitting in the very front row with that long, shiny hair and a winning smile. *That little suck—up!*

"Why yes **Christina** they were! All men who made it to the rank of knighthood were the envy and honor of their town. All women wanted them and men wanted to be them. After all, who wouldn't admire a man in a shiny metal suit defending the weak and innocent everywhere?"

She finished this statement with her right finger pointed high above her head, as if she were poking through to the clouds to heaven, insisting that they listen. The wrinkles on her drawn face all merged into the center around her nose as she spoke, her expression serious. It looked like a raisin pie, like the one Jamie had made during her boredom in the lunchroom one afternoon after collecting every leftover packet of raisins she could find in the kitchen. And there she sat, happily dumping the contents on to the table in front of her, tossing the boxes over her shoulder and smashing the black, prune—like fruit into one large pile with her fists.

But somehow, looking around the dingy barn and the lack of clothing and rotten food provided to her and Aldwin, she felt as if something had been lost in translation; although she couldn't imagine how or why. Miss Legree looked old enough to have been alive during the time of men in shining armor on horseback. But there was certainly nothing noble about a person who treated their underlings with such disregard.

They worked in silence for a few minutes longer with only the faint scratch, scratch, scratch of their brushes and brooms to break through the deafening quiet. A pair of blue birds flew in, their sharp feet skimming the top of Jamie's head as they made a bee line for the rafters. In their beaks they held long, skinny branches and bits of moss. They were building a nest! And as she watched them fly back and forth, feeling the cool breeze from their wings against her cheek a smile broke across her tired face.

"Well, that should do it for now. Lord Destrian is due back any time now for a fresh horse. Let's stop for a minute, okay?"

She tried to nod enthusiastically but her neck felt like a worn out rubber band, stretched too far too soon. Her head flopped around like a dead fish, thrusting her chin into her chest. The pain shot through her causing her back to stiffen as she shuffled over to the corner of the barn, coming to rest on top of an overturned hay bale.

"Water?" He thrust a crude looking canteen at her.

It was warm but oddly refreshing as they both rested their weary bones against the wooden planks behind them. A loud buzzing sound filled her ears as she began to slip off into the world of dreams with her tattered dress clinging to her sweat soaked back. Sharp, stabbing pains in her left leg awoke her with a jolt, just in time to see two huge mosquitoes make off with blood stained stingers, fluttering their wings with glee as they disappeared into the sunset.

The clip—clop of horse's hooves sent a wave of fear throughout her body, causing her to jump straight up; standing at attention. He was back, that bastard in red, cursing loudly as he hurriedly dismounted and then kicked his weary animal, tossing the reins at Jamie while he stood grumpily in the corner, waiting to be undressed. Aldwin fell in stride with the knight, quickly removing his blood stained armor, while nodding sympathetically to all that he said.

"Those pathetic afterlings![10] Do they think themselves clever enough to stand on the soil of my own kingdom and best me at my game? Fonkins![11] They have not heard the last of me! I am Lord Destrian, a man whose blood runs pure with nobility and strength. God will not show mercy…."

He continued to rant and rave, pounding his fists against the wooden planks, causing the entire room to shake with his anger. It seemed to be quite a show he was putting on, kicking the bales of hay around him, even stopping to pick one up and hurl it across the room. Jamie suppressed her giggles and scrubbed the tired horse furiously to avoid eye contact with this raving lunatic. She pitied her barn mate, having to work so closely with someone so

---

[10] *inferiors*
[11] *fools*

unpredictable. But he seemed completely unfazed by these wild outbursts, moving seamlessly from one piece of metal to another, stacking them in a neat pile by his feet.

Soon enough he was gone, leaving in a fury of dust, hay and spit as he cursed the day his fellow jousters were ever born. Aldwin quickly cleaned the dirty armor and then followed the furious knight into his castle, just beyond the barn. There wasn't much Jamie could tell about how the castle was on the inside. All she could see from where she stood was a great stone wall with an enormous door and drawbridge that lowered itself anytime the knight went on a ride. It looked large and impressive from the outside and she let her eyes grow misty with dreams and visions of what the inside must look like.

If the detailed stain glass windows were any indication, gold, silver and goblets encrusted with jewels must lay just beyond that enormous door that took two men to open. An hour passed before Aldwin returned, slightly limping with heavy breath. His face held a strange expression as he assisted her with the final bedding of the animal but he spoke not a word and finished the job quickly.

Finally it was off to bed, but Jamie didn't want to go to sleep, not even after she took her bath and washed her clothes. Aldwin took a bit longer to bathe, hiding himself from her behind the curtain of privacy he had created. She thought it a bit strange that he suddenly decided to hide his nakedness but said nothing. After emptying the pots filled with water on the floor she lay in the middle of the room and stared straight up, looking at the sky.

"What are you doing?" His curiosity finally got the better of him.

"Looking at the stars, aren't they beautiful?"

"I suppose." His voice seemed very far away even though he was standing over her, wrapped in a dry cloth while his clothing dried over the fire.

She ignored his change in attitude, chalking it up to having to spend so much time with someone so evil. *That would have an effect on anybody!*

Scratching her chin she wondered aloud, "could we ever go out into the forest at night, you know, just to see the stars?"

A loud rumble was his response as he shook his head decisively. "No."

"But why not? It's so cramped in here and all we do is work all day!" she complained loudly.

"Lord Destrian would not approve, that's why." That caused her to sit straight up and turn to face him.

"How do you know? Anyways, why would he care? This is our time after work, not his!"

Aldwin shook his head and turned away from her. He was obviously hiding something. But she was too angry to care as she continued to press the issue.

"Look, all I'm saying is we should be able to have some fun. Working in those hot stables all day is exhausting! Wouldn't it be nice," she cooed, moving closer towards him, "to ride out together under the stars with only the moon as our guide?"

"Ride?" this seemed to wake him from his vow of silence. "Do you have any idea what would become of us, should our master discover we stole one of his horses? The pain," he stopped for a moment looking off into the distance, "would be unbearable."

"Oh, poo! We wouldn't be stealing anything, only borrowing. That's no crime!"

"For him it is. Now I'll hear no more of this!" every vein in his neck was throbbing as he spoke. She had never seen him like this, so angry and cold. So Jamie decided to let it go, for now.

But the more she stared up at those big, twinkling stars the more she was determined to find a way to get a better glimpse of them. Back at the girl's home they were never permitted to be outside after dark. And that was one of the things that killed Jamie the most. How she dreamed of sitting under the trees behind the playground, watching their dark shadows dance along the ground; feeling the cool breeze kiss her cheeks as the stars twinkled brightly above like big diamonds on a rich lady's fingers. She may never own a diamond like the one she saw on the lady's hand who rejected her for adoption all those years ago; but she was determined to get a better look at those stars....the diamonds of the sky! After all, they were for everybody. And no amount of money could ever take them away from her.

# Chapter 6

By the time she arose the next morning her roommate was already dressed and ready to walk out the door. Sitting up slowly she observed him, this strange young man with whom she felt a deep connection without knowing why. Last night he had shown her a different side and the reason behind that she could not comprehend. But regardless of what was, today would be better she decided, standing up tentatively and stretching her aching limbs. Today she would make amends for whatever she had done wrong and they would be as old friends again.

But fate had other plans in mind. And before walking out the door Aldwin turned to her and said, "You will be alone in the barn today. I must help inside the castle."

She shook her head to show that she understood but before she could open her mouth to ask any questions he was gone. Hurriedly she dressed, not wanting to anger the knight if he should be up for an early morning practice. Curiosity tingled in her fingertips as she gulped down the glass of milk left for her on the shaky wooden bench. Aldwin had said their master was preparing for a jousting match but for the life of her she could not figure out what that was. She decided to swallow her pride and ask him when they reconvened in the shack later that evening.

The day went slow without him there. With no one to talk to the barn seemed enormous and bare. They never spoke much and she never realized how much his company meant until he was gone. Hour after hour she spent scooping heavy loads of manure into a worn out wheel barrow and replacing the fresh bedding. There were barrels of hay to be stacked but without him to help her there was no way she could get them to the loft at the top of the barn. That will be done tomorrow, she said to herself wiping the mud on her already soiled dress. The holes near the hem had grown larger, making the bottom of the dress sag down to her knees, clinging to a few loose threads on the side of the garment.

With an exasperated sigh she reached down and ripped the sagging hem from her dress. Loose threads hung around her legs, tickling her knees as she tossed the dirt encrusted piece of material over her shoulder. *Oh well*, she thought, her gray eyes scanning the remains of her tattered garment, *it was good while it lasted!*

By mid afternoon her belly was rumbling so loudly it was distracting her from her work. Setting her rake down in the corner she rested her weary bones on a sack of horse feed, waiting for her lunch to be delivered. An hour came and went with no sign of the furious rider who tossed their food at them like they were pigs at the trough before riding away like the devil himself was chasing him.

Jamie couldn't wait any longer to continue her work. Without Aldwin there, she had to do double duty. The time for rest was over. Pulling herself up on trembling legs, she pushed forward, scrubbing down each horse in the barn (there were four in total), dusting off the bags of feed and then finally scrubbing down the area where the animals were bathed with a discarded brush she found hiding in the corner.

Her tongue began to swell with thirst as the sweat rolled down her young back and into her underwear. She looked around for a water spigot or a well of some kind, walking around the outside of the entire barn and along the wall of the red knight's castle. Finally, out of sheer desperation, she knelt down careful not to sit on the wet ground and drank from a puddle untainted by the soapy cleaning water.

The water was warm and turned gray from the massive amounts of dirt and dust that had settled in it. A large, dead beetle floated by while she drank, his stiff black legs sticking straight up in the air as he glided by on his back. After she had her fill she went back to work, praying she wouldn't get sick from drinking the dirty water. Twice more she returned to the filthy puddle during the day as she busied herself around the barn.

Lord Destrian never came for his horses so the time went relatively slow as she only had to wash each animal once instead of twice. And finally when the great ball of yellow heat crept down low in the sky she finished it out by feeding each animal once more and making certain they had fresh bedding in their stalls. How she envied Aldwin, getting to spend all day inside the cool, castle walls, hobnobbing with the local socialites while she toiled away in the heat! *But he has worked their much longer and he deserves a special getaway*, she reminded herself as she dumped the last pile of horse poop into the burn pile on the side of the barn.

Finally her weary legs could take it no longer and as the stars made their appearance she waddled towards the **cruck** with a hungry belly and red rimmed eyes, praying he would be there with some sort of food waiting for her. To her dismay the house was empty and since she had not bothered to learn how to start a fire without matches she spent the night shivering in the dark while the wind howled angrily outside. Even without sleep, never was she more excited to see daylight as it peaked its head in through the many cracks in the roof and walls, making tiny rainbows in the reflection of the water filled pots all over the floor.

She had slept in her clothes to stay warm and as she emerged stinking and starving from the hut she saw him, standing there firewood in hand as he brushed past her, dropping the logs inside the house before making his way to the barn. Jamie followed behind in hot pursuit, not wanting to risk losing him and the food once again. He spoke not a word as they began their morning chores, the sound of hard bristle brushes filling the empty air.

Whatever had happened yesterday was taking its toll on him and as he bent over to pick up a hay bale he grabbed his back, wincing in pain. They had given him a new change of clothes, she noticed, eyeing the fine stitching on his dark brown pants, tailor made to fit his slender form. Gone was the baggy, stained shirt and in its place a heavy cotton pull over that stood straight and starched, clinging to his youthful body as he bent over the bales.

"You got new shoes," she noted aloud, nodding in approval at the shiny leather moccasins covering his feet.

He said nothing, but turned slowly and sat down on the packed hay, his face pale. Jamie walked over to study him. Sympathy was not her strong suit, especially since she was the one forced to work all day while he got to stay inside with new clothes to boot!

Shaking her head she looked around the already clean barn, clean from her countless hours of scrubbing and said, "I'm hungry. You weren't here yesterday so they didn't bring me anything to eat."

Minutes passed as they sat in silence while she stared at him and he stared at the floor. A pounding in her head like two men slamming sledge hammers against a metal bell had started, keeping beat with the rumbling in her empty stomach. Whatever patience she was pretending to have for the sake of being polite was rapidly disappearing. Here he showed up with new clothes and a full stomach while she spent the day starving and the night freezing, having nothing but puddle water to keep her from passing out. *And now he was stopping because his back hurt?*

"Come on, let's go," she said coldly, standing up, nudging him on. He ignored her, turning his face to the side, gasping for breath.

"Look, I'm tired too," Jamie said softly, trying another angle, "but if we don't do something we're gonna get in trouble, remember?" Still, he did not move.

With disgusted sigh she towered over him, poking at his shoulder. "Get up will you? I'm hungry and tired but you don't hear me complaining! And you got to spend the day in the castle and got new clothes too!"

He became animated now, turning towards her, his green eyes glassy. "You don't know what you are talking about Miss Jamie. And if you don't mind can you please just leave me alone?"

She walked away in a huff to the other side of the barn, leaving him to lick his wounds. A few minutes later he was up and at it, moving at a snail's pace while she, sick and irritated, worked circles around him. They ate lunch separately as she couldn't stand to sit there and stare at the sad expression on his face. *What does he have to be sad about? I would give anything to be in the castle instead of out here....even if it is with that mean old knight!*

That evening was much of the same, the two of them sitting together, staring silently at the fire while the rain patted softly on the roof and in the pots on the floor. It was too cold to sit very far away from the fire and so they bore an uncomfortable existence, each doing their level best not to speak to each other while snuggling ever closer to ward off the wet freeze that was settling in.

At last she could stand it no longer and wrapping the threadbare blanket around her shoulders she walked outside, staring up at the glittering, white balls in the sky. The moon was still unusually thin and this bothered her to no end. Whatever lesson she was suppose to be learning here wasn't working out and she was anxious to return to the museum under the sleep of a full moon. What had started out as a promising friendship had turned to dust and now she was forced to rely on someone who wouldn't even speak to her, let alone guide her to the path of knowledge and fulfillment.

But despite her anger she was forced to return quickly as the icy winds gnawed at her fragile bones, piercing the almost non—existent blanket. She stood in the doorway, unsure of where to go or how to go about it. He was now lying directly in front of the fire, resting comfortably as could be on his lumpy mattress. A soft snore emerged from his throat, whistling out his nostrils as he shivered in his sleep.

And as she watched him sleep so peacefully, she wondered if she had been too hard on him. With a belly full of food and fresh water it was easier to think clearly and as his thin figure rose and fell under the torn gunny sack he used for a blanket, she made up her mind to make things right. After all, he was the only person she knew and was willing to help her. Gently, she reached out and stroked his back as a soft smile played her lips. *He really wasn't so bad!*

But her good intentions were cut short with an angry smack across the face. Aldwin had awoken when she touched him and responded by leaping out of bed and striking her, hard. His nostrils flared as he loomed over her crouched form. Jamie's mouth flew open in a state of silent protest but he was in no mood to render an apology. Instead he leaped forward, stopping an inch in front of her shocked face. Never had he seemed so intimidating with his shoulders spread wide as an eagle's and his fists clenched tightly by his side.

"Don't ever do that again! Understand?!? You don't know….." A muscular finger was pointing directly in her face as emerald eyes burned holes through her trembling frame.

Tears sprang to her eyes, making his sinewy figure blur in front of her. He either wouldn't or couldn't finish his statement and in one fluid motion spun around, lying back in front of the fire. Jamie moved back slowly towards her bed where she spent the night, watering the straw with salty tears until she fell asleep from exhaustion. She didn't understand what was going on with him, or why he was so angry with her. It just didn't make any sense.

But whatever was going to happen next she didn't want to be any part of and she made up her mind right then and there to steal a horse and ride far away into the forest and hide out until the moon became full again. Then they would be rid of her and she of them. And then the red knight and Aldwin could enjoy each other's company in the castle, the stable, wherever. *Yes*, she decided snuggling deeper under the skimpy quilt, *that's exactly what I'm going to do!*

# **Chapter 7**

"Take this beast and be finished with him by the time I return!"

Jamie nodded to show that she understood; eyes downcast as the irritable man in metal pushed past her and towards the newly saddled stallion. She hid her cheek, still sore and red from the angry smack she received last night with a clump of loose, unwashed hair. After a moment of struggling to mount the frightened animal he called to Aldwin for assistance. Jamie smirked in spite of herself. *That horse is smarter than all of us!*

"Over here, boy! Bend your back so that you may prove yourself useful yet!"

Without a word the young man got on all fours next to the thrashing horse, tucking his chin to his chest, lest he be struck unconscious by one of the prancing hooves that stomped dangerously close to his head. Grunting heavily, the red knight placed both feet on top of the boy's tender back and stood for a moment, adjusting his saddle, while Aldwin shook, struggling to hold the massive combined weight of the man and his armor. Peeking out from behind the horse she was brushing, Jamie watched with baited breath as Aldwin's skinny arms trembled and heavy sweat began to drip from the tip of his nose, forming a small puddle in the dirt below.

"Straighten your back boy," the knight yelled, digging his metal heel into the young man's back, laughing out loud as his servant groaned under the tremendous pressure.

Aldwin's mouth flew open as he began to pant from exhaustion, waiting for the knight to mount. He was too young and small to handle such a heavy burden. And soon his body would give way causing significant damage. Looking down and noticing the boy's pain the red knight smiled wickedly.

"Feeling the pressure eh boy? You should be stronger than that after what you endured in the castle!"

It was at that moment Jamie realized that Aldwin was not being given special treatment by Lord Destrian, but in fact was being terrorized by him. *If he would do this in front of me, God only knows what he went through in the castle that night in secret!* A shiver went down her spine as she watched him struggle to hold his master's weight. It seemed like an impossible task but after what seemed like an eternity, the haughty knight mounted his steed and galloped off into the morning sun rise.

The moment he was out of sight Aldwin collapsed on the barn floor, moaning in agony. Rolling himself into a protective ball he huddled, face down, in the corner, pressing his face into the bristly bales of fresh hay that were due to be stacked in the loft. Jamie ran over to his quivering form, longing to reach out and comfort him. She could relate to what he was going through, the fear, the pain, the embarrassment were all things she had faced at the orphanage at the hands of others.

"Oh wow, how pretty!"

"Isn't it though?"

"I just said that didn't I?"

"How could you afford this?"

"A girl has her ways...."

It was time for the grooming class at the girl's home and Miss Legree had spared no expense with various posters and recycled pictures that showed how to make one's self positively irresistible. The classroom was abuzz with activity as each girl made her way up to the front of the room to admire the one girl who was chosen to go with the headmistress in to town for a proper make-over. Each year it was someone different. Whoever sucked up the most was chosen. And since the favored girls were so quickly adopted out, each year there was an opening for a new apple polisher to take center stage.

"Now girls I know you are excited but please take your seats so the lesson can begin."

Miss Legree looked unusually dapper that morning. True, she was still sporting the ankle length black dress that came up to her chin and tickled her wrists, but her hair which was normally pulled straight back with a mass of rusty bobby pins was hanging loose with long, soft waves and her face was painted up nicely, like a proper old woman should look. And as Jamie stared at her, above the sea of eager faces and hands that shot straight up into the air with a flurry of questions she realized there was a beauty to this woman, one she had never noticed before.

"Take your brush, I have provided one for you on your desks, and brush your hair until it shines!"

"How will we know when it shines?" asked an enthusiastic red head in the front row.

"One hundred strokes per night. That will give you that soft manageable look every woman desires."

Jamie sat and stared at the dirty brush with the broken handle in front of her. There was no way she was running that through her hair! It looked as if it had been pulled out of a garbage can and with the orphanage's limited budget, it just might have. And as the other girls inquired about make—up and shoe polishing, Jamie let her mind wander to the couple who had refused to adopt her after they saw her. Granted, she was dirty with sticks in her hair from playing in the woods behind the playground; but what young girl wouldn't want to go outside and play? Wasn't that normal? This couldn't be it, sitting around all day brushing your hair and applying make—up in hopes of pleasing someone else.

"I see you haven't touched your brush," Miss Legree had snuck up behind her as she was contemplating these things and gripped her shoulder with menacing force.

Jamie glared up at her, refusing to back down. This was stupid. And there was no way someone could convince her otherwise. Then suddenly with a tremendous whoosh she was escorted to the front of the classroom, stumbling to keep pace with the headmistress on a mission. Standing in front of the room full of girls, she crossed her arms and thrust her chin high in the air. *There was no way this lady was going to steal any more of her dignity!*

"Girls," her voice sounded like fingernails down a chalk board as her bony fingers dug deep into Jamie's shoulders. "I would just like to point out that young Jamie here has chosen not to cooperate with our grooming tutorial."

Giggles were heard starting from the back row and slowly rippling forward. They all knew what was coming; her embarrassment. It had happened often enough for God's sake.

"Now, keep in mind I show you these things not because they will benefit me, but because I want only the best for you. Being adopted is not an easy thing. After all, there are plenty of options for potential parents to choose from."

She gestured around the room when she said this, pointing to each girl with her long, bony fingernails. They all shook their heads to show that they understood.

"Young Jamie here was already passed up for adoption once. Can anyone guess the reason why?"

Hands shot up all around the room. Everyone was eager to play their part in her humiliation. The first one to speak was the pretty, blond girl with sparkling blue eyes in the second row.

"Because she's so mean?"

"Or maybe because she acts like a boy?" chimed in another with mischievous brown eyes. High pitched laughter echoed throughout the room.

"All good answers but, no. The reason they rejected her was because of her appearance. She came into my office covered with dirt and leaves in her hair! Now I ask you class, can you imagine any respectable couple wanting to adopt someone like that? Never mind her personality, or record of bad behavior."

And as she stood there, facing all those girls, her cheeks flamed pink as she fought back tears. They were taking turns throwing stones at her and it hurt, bad. But there was no way she could let them see that, no way she could let them win. So, she did what she always did; hid it all away and put on a brave face until she was alone and could cry it out until her lungs burst.

After a few minutes Aldwin sat up, gasping for air. Jamie handed him a glass of warm water from the bucket he kept for them to drink from during the day. He accepted it gratefully, a quick smile crossing his face as he gulped it down.

"Are you okay?"

She knew she probably shouldn't speak to him. That seemed to be the last thing he wanted. But seeing his suffering she just couldn't help herself. He bowed his head and slammed the cup down on the floor before turning to acknowledge her. There was a pain in his eyes she had seen only once before, when looking in the mirror. That kind of pain that made you stare at yourself and wonder, who am I? It startled her but as they locked eyes she knew then that they would be the best of friends no matter what the circumstance. They shared something few others could relate to. And with a twinkle in his eye, Aldwin put out his hand as a sign of peaceful surrender. She grabbed his hand and helped pull him to his feet.

Together they stood in the barn, facing each other, not speaking in words but with their hearts. A warm feeling washed over Jamie and before she realized it, she was hugging him with all her might, sobbing uncontrollably. Big alligator tears rolled down her cheeks, staining his new shirt as he held her close in the early morning light. Shadows crossed over her first hiding, then illuminating, the years of pain that flowed down her face.

Resting her head against his chest and feeling the tip of his sharp chin settle on top of her head the two souls became one, sharing a moment no one could ever take away from them. And as the horse's whinnied in the background and the smell of manure filled the air, a gentle hand stroked her red cheek, apologizing without speech for what had transpired the night before. And for the first time since she had been there, a glimmer of aspiration was illuminated in her soul. *Perhaps there was hope yet!*

# **Chapter 8**

Several days passed before she mentioned the idea of leaving for the night on horseback again. During that time they carried on the same routine of caring for the horses, cleaning the barn and stacking the new bags of feed and hay that came in. The red knight had not taken Aldwin away for the night since then and Jamie had stopped her quest in learning how to remove the knight's armor. She didn't want to be near him; the way he smiled with those brown, slimy teeth and dark eyes that looked like two holes leading into a bottomless pit gave her the creeps.

Their nights together fell in to a sort of comical routine, as they switched places bathing, washing clothes and emptying out the broken pots that caught the rain water on the floor of the hut with a sort of timed rhythm. Words between them were few but after what happened in the barn it didn't really seem necessary anymore. Sitting next to each other in front of the roaring fire, sipping warm milk and chewing on left over jerky they would catch each other's eye and simply smile.

It was raining that night; pouring more like it. And as the trees wailed outside their tiny **cruck** a sort of tension was building inside those four walls; one that could be contained no longer. Turning her face towards him, she studied the contours of his profile in the flickering flames. His face was smooth and lean with high cheek bones standing out stiffly under sparkling green eyes. Fine lines ran from the sides of his long nose to the edges of his mouth in a perfect arch shape. And in his own way, he was beautiful.

"How old are you?" she asked, watching his unmoving torso catch the shadows of light that played across the fireplace.

"Sixteen."

Well! That was older than what she had originally expected. But then again Jamie had never met anyone who was sixteen years old so she didn't know what they should really look like. The only people she had known were the other girls in the orphanage who were all younger than her and Miss Legree who was clearly decades older than she. He sensed her puzzlement, noting her wrinkled brow and puckered, pink mouth.

"You were expecting a different answer then?"

"No," she struggled to give the right response, "it's not that it's just…..I thought you were younger that's all," she finished lamely, shrugging her shoulders as a sign of utter bewilderment.

"Why are you here?" The question took her completely off guard as the next rational thing for him to ask would be her age.

"What do you mean? Now? Because it's dark and we need to sleep."

A low gurgling sound escaped his throat as his lips pursed tightly together. Color flooded to his cheeks as he bowed his head and looked away with shaking shoulders. He was laughing at her!

"Hey!" Jamie yelled in protest, shoving against his solid figure, watching in amazement at the muscles ripple in his arms as he attempted to balance himself. Finally he composed himself and turned to face her, cheeks still enflamed with guilt.

"Okay, okay, sorry about that! Look, what I meant to ask was…..why did Lord Destrian bring you here? What did you do wrong?"

"I didn't do anything wrong," she snuffed haughtily.

He considered her answer, tilting his head to the side, observing the new hole in the roof above them.

"Well then, how did you meet?"

"Uhhhhh," this question posed a real problem for her. She couldn't tell where they really met, inside the museum. "I accidently ran out in front of his horse when he was fighting another knight and it threw him off….."

Aldwin raised his hand and nodded his head to show that he understood.

"So you got in his way and robbed him of a victory?"

Jamie shook her head. She had never thought of it like that before. The only thing going through her mind at the time was the desperate need to be noticed before the sun rose.

"How about you?" Now it was his turn to confess.

"My father owed a great deal of money and could not pay it off before he died."

"But what does that have to do with you?"

"Well, I don't know where you come from but here, when a man owes a debt that he cannot pay he either sells everything he owns to make payment, or sells himself into slavery. We didn't have anything of value. Just the clothes on our backs and one ox that did the ploughing."

She considered his answer while drumming her fingers on the hard wooden floor.

"So how long have you been his servant?"

"Since I was five years old. But one day I will be a free man! And then," his features became illuminated as he leaned forward, brimming with excitement, "I will buy my own plot of land and my own oxen and start farming. Of course I will need to save up enough money for a wife and a family."

Jamie stared into his eyes as he spoke, showing that she was paying careful attention to everything that was said. This was the first time they had really opened up to each other and she did not want it to end. But her mind wandered back to the forest and the star light sky that covered them like a canopy, just waiting to be explored.

"What about you miss Jamie? What do you intend to do when you are free?"

The thought struck her as funny because she had never thought of herself as being a slave to anything. In fact, she had worked very hard to not fall in line with the norm and do things her own way. But there was one thing she still desired more than anything else in the world.

"I want to find a mother—parents who will adopt me and take me to live with them forever."

"So you want to be loved?"

Jamie smiled in response. She had never considered love to be the one thing she was chasing. But when he said it, it all made perfect sense.

"Now then," he said with an air of dignity about him, "what is it you really want to ask me?"

"What do you mean?"

"You didn't start talking to me just to ask how old I was."

He was right. And the knowingness showed all over his face as he tossed his head like a spirited horse, allowing the stray pieces of light brown hair to fall carelessly in his eyes. Taking a deep breath and closing her eyes she said what had been on her mind for the past several days.

"Can we go riding out to the forest to see the stars? And if you say no," she added, noticing the wrinkles form between his eyebrows, "I'll just go by myself."

Silence filled the room. Jamie's heart pounded so loudly it pulsated in her ear drums. She knew he would be angry. The last time she brought this up he got very upset. But that was days ago and maybe now he would be in a better mood. Maybe.

"I thought we already settled this." His voice was stern and unbending.

"No. You made up your mind a long time ago. But for me," her eyes scanned the run down hovel, "I'm getting sick and tired of doing nothing but working all day and then having to stay here all night like a prisoner. Maybe that's okay with you, but I'm bored!"

Every bone in his neck popped as he twisted his neck all the way around, staring at the opposite wall. It had caved in and been patched with mud and sap several times but still kept coming undone. The pots on the floor, he noted, needed to be dumped out soon or else they would overflow.

"You will go without me if I say no?"

She shook her head yes. Jamie didn't really want to go by herself. She had been alone her entire life and it would be fun to have someone along who knew the area and could chat with as they rode. Aldwin picked up a piece of rogue straw that had escaped from the bedding and tossed it into the fire, watching it ignite and burn up instantly.

He was considering her proposal. She could tell by the way his eyes were darting back and forth and the way his fingers were turning white as he folded his hand together, staring blankly ahead. Long, throbbing veins ran from the back of his knuckles all the way up to his bicep. She could only guess how many times the red knight had used him as a footstool for him to develop those muscles.

"Do you know how to ride?"

"I know how to saddle them up."

The only time she had been on top of one of those animals was when the red knight had taken her as his hostage. She remembered all the jarring and bumping around as she clung to the beast's mane trying desperately not to fall off. And those painful sores on the insides her thighs…yikes! She needed him and he knew that.

Standing up slowly he fiddled with his belt before going over to the corner to grab the one, thin blanket he owned. After tossing it to her, he put his old shirt under his new shirt and then sat down to put on his fancy new shoes. Jamie looked down at the blanket, confused.

"What do I need this for?"

"Because it gets cold at night and since you don't have any proper clothes," he added, eyeing her disheveled dress from the orphanage, "this will have to do."

And as he ushered her out the door, the rain suddenly stopped as if signaling its approval with what they were doing. She turned her back to him and wrapped the cloth tightly around her shoulders as a smile claimed her face. *They were finally going to go riding under the stars!*

# Chapter 9

"But why can't I ride my own horse?"

Quietly as doves they had stole away into the barn, saddling and then mounting the tired, swaybacked animal. Aldwin sat in front, holding the reigns firmly as his eyes scanned the perimeter for any sign of movement. All it would take was one person to see them, a guard, a curios peasant, or even Lord Destrian himself for the jig to be up. He had endured unspeakable things at the hand of the red knight and so he weighed the risk carefully as they slowly walked out of the barn and around the castle.

"Be silent until we are away from the castle," he whispered fiercely, "if anyone should see us...."

Jamie pressed her head against his back and nodded to show that she understood. He sat head and shoulders above her, with muscles tensed as the cool night air whistled in their ears. It was too dark to see anything. In fact she wondered how he managed to know where everything was as they maneuvered carefully around random work benches and sharp tools that littered the ground on the side of the drawbridge.

*What a mess!* She thought, shaking her head at the sight of it. It seemed strange that the red knight was so particular about the state of his animals but gave little thought to the cleanliness of his castle grounds. Jamie had always wanted to see the castle in the light of day, in all its glory. The one opportunity she had was when she was brought their forcibly on horseback. It had been daylight then, but her fear and pain prevented her from drinking in the scenery as she would have liked.

"Wrap your arms around me tight and hold on!"

Without another word they sped off, as he dug his heels into the soft side of the animal, urging them onwards. Jamie closed her eyes and held on for dear life. The last time she had been on a horse it had not ended so well for her but this time, she determined, it would be much better.

"Relax," he breathed, taking long gulps of air to keep in rhythm of the stallion's canter, "don't fight the rhythm of the horse or else you will be sore in the morning!"

Fearfully she followed his instructions, first by loosening the grip with her legs and sitting back on the animal like he was. Her breath was the next to come in long, frightful gasps from holding it for so long and then her neck, resting it gently against his broad shoulders. It was really quite peaceful on top of this creature, feeling the wind in her face and smelling the tall grasses around them. But most importantly, they were away from that awful barn with all those offensive odors and redundant behavior of cleaning, brushing and stacking bags and bags of feed and bales of new hay.

At long last she trusted him enough to open her eyes and take in the world around them. Tall, looming trees that entwined overhead, blocking out the moonlight stretched out in front of them; their thick, black branches curving and bending like an old woman's spine as they reached towards the sky with purpose. A loud hooting sound followed by the flapping of wings caused her to jump out of her skin as the sound echoed throughout the woods.

"It's just an owl," Aldwin said soothingly, feeling her body jolt in time with the music of the forest, "see?"

His white sleeve served as a point of reference as Jamie followed the length of it with her eyes to the branch where a fat bird with what appeared to be strange, pointed ears sticking out of the top of its head sat, staring back at them. Its eyes were round as saucers, almost glowing in the dim light of the moon that managed to sneak through the matted leaves. Never had Jamie seen a creature like that before, up close and personal. Most of the things she knew about were from the pages of a weathered book, or from the posters shown in class by Miss Legree.

"It's so dark." This wasn't anything like she had expected.

"Give me but a moment and I'll show you something wonderful."

They rode listening to the faint whisper of the wind as it rustled the leaves and swayed the branches of the trees overhead. It sounded like an eerie melody fit for Halloween with all the moans and groans mixed with the crunching of the sticks under the horse's hooves. They had celebrated Halloween at the orphanage, only Miss Legree called it a "fall festival" since it was considered by some to be the holiday of the devil.

Everyone got dressed up for the occasion, using recycled costumes that were discarded from the stores the year before. Miss Legree did a fair amount of trash picking in an attempt to show them a good time. Of course all the costumes were made for younger children as the tradition went and so Jamie often found herself the only one with nothing to wear.

They would put on a parade of sorts, with each girl taking her turn in front of everyone else to show what she was wearing. Then everybody would ooh and ahh as they took center stage, twirling around like a prima ballerina. Of course the headmistress never participated in the game of dressing up, but she did allow the girls to use some of her old make—up and frazzled brushes on this special occasion to put the finishing touches on their outfits.

"And what are you suppose to be?" the old woman would ask each girl as they stepped in front of the group, even if it was painful obvious.

"I'm a princess!"

"A ballerina!"

"A fairy with sparkly wings!"

And the list went on and on as Jamie sat in the corner, tugging at the hem of her state issued uniform. She felt a hard knot form in the pit of her stomach, listening to them all laugh around her, stroking each other's hair and admiring each other's outfits. No one ever asked her to join the parade. Why bother? She didn't have a costume and even if she did she wouldn't be caught dead up there, prancing around like a jackass.

"All right now girls, it's time to play our party games!" The old mistress clapped her withered hands together like a trained seal as everyone lined up in front of the apple bob.

One year Jamie had grown tired of sitting in the corner and decided to join in fun and festivities. And so with a reluctant sigh, she lined up behind the other girls and waited for her turn to bob for apples. It seemed like great fun, as each child ahead of her squealed with delight when they came up with a shiny, red apple between their teeth. Some picked it up by the stem and saved their faces; others dove right in and came up soaking wet with bits of the fruit in their mouth.

Finally it was Jamie's turn and she assumed the position, kneeling down with her hands behind her back in front of the water filled tub. She eyed each remaining piece of fruit, zeroing in on the ones with the longest stems. Nimbly she leaned over and opened her mouth wide, flicking them around with her tongue until she cornered one. With a mischievous smile she bit down on the stem and tried to lift her head back only to find that she couldn't move. The other girls had crowded around her while Miss Legree was distracted and were pushing her head down, under the water.

Jamie flailed around, reaching back and trying to pull their angry little fingers off the back of her neck. She couldn't breathe and as desperation set in, she twisted her entire body around until they were forced to let go, pulling several painful chunks of hair with them. Now her entire back was soaked and as she stood up she was met with a harsh smack across her cheek.

"Just look at what you've done!" It was the headmistress. Apparently she had noticed something was wrong when everyone started yelling all at once. "You've ruined it, just ruined it!" she shrieked, pointing at the puddles of water all over the floor.

There was no point in saying anything. She would not be believed anyways. And without a word Jamie leaned over and with all the strength she could muster, dumped over the entire apple bob tub before walking out of the room.

"Here it is!"

They had reached a clearing in the trees and as she dismounted the bright moon beams nearly blinded her, causing her to cup her hands around her eyes as she looked up and around. They were standing in the center of a perfect, bare circle with nothing but the cool grass and rows of brightly colored flowers scattered all around. Woodland creatures peaked out from the surrounding trees, noses twitching as they watched with curious eyes.

For some reason the grass was short here, in the circle, almost as if someone had cut it that way. Tilting her head back she gasped in awe of the big, bright, glorious stars that shone in the velvety purple sky. Never had she seen anything so beautiful, not even in her wildest dreams could she have imagined how perfect this all could be.

"Come. Sit."

He ushered her on to the plush grass that felt like silk under her fingertips. Jamie inhaled deeply, smelling everything and nothing all at once. Suddenly the moon drifted into their field of vision, standing directly over them, illuminating the entire circle brighter than the sun.

"This must be what heaven's like, or so the good father's say." She scratcher her head as he spoke.

"What good father? I thought you said your father died."

"He did. I meant the priest. We call them father."

"Why?"

"A sign of respect I suppose."

Jamie didn't really get what he was talking about. She had never heard of the Catholic religion, in fact she had never heard of any religion, only the Bible that Miss Legree read passages from when the mood struck her. It didn't matter though. This was a perfect night, something for the story books. Laying back Jamie rubbed herself around like a sugar coated cookie, feeling the soft, green blades brush against her cheek.

"I wish we could stay here forever!"

"Me too. Maybe build a house here." At last he was finally using his imagination, something Jamie could appreciate.

"Right here? In this circle? How magical!"

He chuckled softly, watching her enjoy every moment of this newfound freedom. Together they lay, side by side, watching the moon sneak slowly across the sky and the stars fade from sight. Few words were exchanged as they felt the pulsating of each other's hearts through their shoulders pressed tightly together on the forest floor.

"We should return soon. It will be daylight."

Quickly they mounted their sleeping horse and made their way back to the stable. The castle looked magnificent in the early morning light. Soft hues of purple and orange served as a perfect backdrop for the regal stone masterpiece that spread out farther than the city block that held the museum. The center was a square shape with a big, gaping mouth that served as the drawbridge. On the sides were various pillar shaped stone towers that stood taller than anything she had ever seen before. There were various stain glass windows that covered the pillar towers and at the top they resembled crowns with their jagged, square shaped cuts.

"Ooooh! I would love to see inside of it!" Jamie's imagination was going wild with the endless possibilities that lay in front of her.

"No you don't. You don't ever want to see the inside of that," he said, motioning towards the stone mansion, "the price you will pay is more than you can imagine."

Jamie nodded solemnly to show that she understood, even though she didn't. They were in luck as they rounded the bend and into the barn. No one was up yet and their secret was still safe. And by the time they finished scrubbing down the animal and putting everything away, a ferocious yawn fought its way to Jamie's mouth, signaling her exhaustion.

"I'm so tired! I don't know how we are going to work all day now!"

"We don't have to," his words came like music to her ears, "Lord Destrian does not ride on Sundays per his Christian oaths."

It made no sense to Jamie but for once she did not care. Any reason she was given to sleep in was fine by her. And as they staggered towards the **cruck**, linked arm in arm, her weary eyes acknowledged Aldwin gratefully as he tended to the fire and emptied the floor pots.

"I take it you had a good time then, m'lady?"

But his only response was a gentle snore, as her body had slipped into a deep slumber before her head hit the pillow. Smiling, he turned back to the fire, adding more wood and bits of dry paper. It would be morning soon and if the house was to remain warm throughout the day, they would need more kindling.

# Chapter 10

"Hot today isn't it?"

Jamie shook her head up and down in response, her swollen tongue hanging out of her mouth as she tossed pitchfork after pitchfork of hay over her shoulder and into the freshly scrubbed stalls. It was the beginning of the week which meant each stall had to be stripped bare and scrubbed until it shone, only to be refilled with more hay and animal feed. In addition, the horses had to be removed from their stalls and scrubbed down even though they had not been ridden before being returned to their wooden cubbies.

A cracked wooden cup was thrust in her sweaty face, dribbling down the sides as she gulped it down, smiling gratefully. They worked side-by-side, never daring to speak aloud of the wonderful adventures they had indulged in the night before. Warm air blew slow and steady through the barn, stirring up more dirt as they fought valiantly to keep everything clean.

"What did you do before I got here?"

It was a question that had been plaguing Jamie's mind all morning as they bent over to clean, feeling the splinters in their knee caps and the twinge in their lower backs as they reached above their head to swat away cobwebs and pesky flies that buzzed around their ears.

"I worked with another boy, another **theow** of Lord Destrian."

"Oh," her mind was sluggish from the crippling heat, "but what happened to him?"

At first he didn't respond, staring intensely at the wooden plank in front of him, letting the soap and water saturate the board before wiping it down.

"He went to live in the castle."

Jamie scoffed in disgust, "Well lucky him! Wish I could go live in the castle and not have to do this anymore!"

Aldwin shook his head but said nothing, turning his attention towards the impatient animal tied to the post behind him. The animal tossed his head back and blew air out loudly through his nose. He wasn't too fond of the heat either, Jamie noted, dipping her brush back into the bucket of sudsy water.

"Were you friends with him—the boy you worked with in the barn?"

Aldwin nodded his head slowly, "Something like that."

"So do you still get to see him?" He shook his head "no" not daring to make eye contact with her.

"Why not?" She needed some distraction from this God awful work but it always seemed she was the one striking up all the conversations.

Aldwin did not answer her, pretending to be too engrossed in the new barrels of hay that had just arrived. Turning his back to her, he exited the stall and began to stack them all in neat piles by the pulley system near the loft. An off key tune escaped his lips as he worked, ignoring the penetrating stare behind him. Jamie continued to work, but kept her gaze on him. He was hiding something and she intended to find out what!

At long last he was forced to turn around, casting a sideways glance to the floor as he brushed past her in the stall.

"Well?" Jamie had no intention of letting this go.

"Well what?"

He was putting off the inevitable. But this was a game she knew all too well. In the girl's home Miss Legree thrived on excluding her from their discussion, purposefully ignoring her raised hand during class as her beady eyes scanned the room, hopeful that someone else would ask a question. It got so bad that Jamie stopped asking all together, tired of feeling the ache in her shoulder from keeping her hand up for so long.

There had been one particular instance where the headmistress had looked right at her. It was like locking eyes with the devil himself, staring into those dark, wavering pools to which there seemed to be no end. It was at that moment, when the class fell silent and everyone turned to look at her that she realized this woman hated her. Before she had been under the assumption that she was just not being seen, or that it was just not a good time for questions. And now…..

"Well, why don't you ever talk to him anymore—your friend?"

She wasn't going to stop. He could see that now. With a reluctant sigh he stopped scrubbing, his hands hardening around the brush until his knuckles turned white as he spoke.

"He was sold. Thrown out like an old shoe. That's what he does, the red knight. After he tires of someone they are gone. Just like that. No telling, it just happens. And then," his voice grew tight as he continued, letting the pain spill out through his words, "it's like that person was never here. You are forbidden to speak of them and if you do the beating you will get…."

He couldn't go on any more. Without another word he threw down his brush, letting it clatter noisily on the floor before walking off; leaving her alone with her thoughts. She hadn't meant to upset him. But it seemed like they couldn't talk about anything regarding the castle without him getting irritable. And what else was there to speak of? Day and night they cleaned animal poop and wiped down their sweaty backs. That wasn't exactly anything to write home about.

The minutes seemed like hours before he finally returned with two fresh buckets of water in tow. The rest of the day dragged on as they ate their meager lunch in silence, while she studied the courting patterns of two flies that hovered around their food. Several days' worth of sweat and dirt had buried themselves in her scalp, causing her to itch fiercely. And as she scratched at her head, her eyes wandered down to the rags she was wearing. There wasn't much left to that state issued dress from the orphanage. It was stained and torn beyond repair despite her repeated attempts to clean it so carefully in the evening by the light of the fire with a bar of sweet smelling soap.

"I'll get us an extra bucket of water tonight," he said, taking pity on her.

"It hurts," she wined, digging deeper between the hair follicles with her dirty fingernails.

A large chunk of dirt came loose as she was clawing at her head and fell in her lap. To her surprise the dirt had legs and scampered away quickly as she stared at it in awe. *A bug, a real bug had been living in her hair and she didn't even know it?* A gagging sensation started at the back of her throat and before she knew it, Aldwin was holding her up while she dry heaved in the corner.

Later that evening while they were resting comfortably by the fire, their clothing and hair scrubbed clean, Aldwin stole quietly away while Jamie sat staring into the flickering flames of the roaring fire. She was taking special note of how the fires she had seen in pictures differed from the real ones. Tilting her head to the side she let the red, orange and blue flecks all blend together into one gloriously warm rainbow.

"Did you ever notice how fires in pictures are always colored all red, but in real life they have so many different colors to them?"

Silence. Perhaps he was contemplating the depth of her question. After all, it wasn't every day someone mentioned the differing hues of a fire. Smiling she turned to see what it was that had him so engrossed he could not think of an answer. Water dripped steadily into the pots covering the bare floor, leading up to a creaky, half—closed door. He was gone.

She looked around one more time just to be sure; not that there was any place to hide in that tiny hut they inhabited. Icy winds tore through the cracks in the ceiling and the walls, blowing aside the hanging sheet they used for privacy while bathing. The pile of hay in the corner where she slept lay empty and the pots sang loudly, filled to the brim with fat drops of rain as they reflected the vacancy of the bench and chair over in the corner.

Scratching her head she turned around to face the fire once more. Maybe he had to go and get more firewood. But no, they had plenty; she realized eyeballing the large stack next to the crudely shaped hearth. Perhaps he had to tend to the red knight this evening. Deep in her heart she hoped that was not the case. Last time he had to do that he was a terrible grump the next day.

The minutes flew by quickly and soon she realized how tired she was, rubbing the ache out of her arms and her thighs with her bruised fingertips. *Maybe went to the castle for something and got lost in one of the many rooms and corridors, she thought,* shaking her head at the silliness of the idea. Aldwin had been a servant to the knight long before she came along. She didn't know how many times he had actually been inside the castle, but she was certain he would not get lost. Not after the way he navigated their trip to the forest in the pitch darkness so beautifully.

Slowly, her body relaxed, sinking down closer to the mattress in front of the fire. *I'll just close my eyes for a minute*, she told herself, *just a minute and then I'll get up and search for him myself!* And as the moon climbed high in the sky, peering in through the many openings in the roof, her mind drifted away to blissful places with dreams sweeter than honey to soothe her tortured soul.

"M'lady? M'lady? Miss Jamie?"

She had slept the entire night away without even realizing it. Cursing her own laziness, she sat straight up, rubbing her eyes to wipe away the fog and hard, crusty things that formed in the corners. The sun still slept, but the purple and orange rays that were peeking their bashful faces out over the horizon urged her upwards with promising results. Today wouldn't be as hot, she noted, wrapping the thin blanket around her shoulders. Usually it was warm by this time but the nip in the air had stayed, lingering in the darkened room as the fire shadows danced on the wall.

"Drink your milk quickly and get dressed. Lord Destrian requires us to be ready and at his side early this morning for his jousting tournament."

Jamie nodded even though she didn't understand. To her it was all the same, each day merging into the next with the cleaning of the barn and the scrubbing and feeding of the animals. Rising quickly she limped over to the table, her legs still sore from all the squatting and stretching they had done the day before. The glass of milk stood in its usual place in the same cracked mug with a missing handle. But there was something else. Sitting next to it was a large package wrapped in brown paper and held together with string. Curiously she poked at it, wondering what it could be.

"Open it." He stood across the table from her, his eyes glittering as if he was keeping a special king of secret.

Carefully she opened it, sliding off the string first and then unfolding the paper with trembling hands. A green piece of folded material was staring her in the face. Her mouth flew open, not knowing what it was or how to react. Seeing her distress Aldwin walked over and unfolded it for her. Jamie gasped when she saw what it was. A dress, a beautiful, long green dress with embroidered details on the cuffs and the collar was hanging from his fingertips.

"Who, what is this for?"

He smiled, seeing her obvious pleasure. "It is for you m'lady, to wear to the joust this morning."

Fighting back tears Jamie took the dress from him and put it on. It felt soft and clean against her skin and smelled of fresh soap. And when she emerged from behind the privacy sheet he was standing there, waiting. She walked towards him, eyes downcast, giddy as a schoolgirl.

"Stop," he commanded, holding up his hand, "now turn around."

She obeyed without question, spinning slowly, allowing the heavy cotton skirt to billow out around her ankles.

"It fits. But what do you think?"

Jamie smiled, feeling a strange sensation overwhelm her. It started in her stomach and then moved to her chest and then her eyes. And before she knew it, tears were streaming down her cheeks while she hugged him close and whispered the words *thank you* in his ear. It was the first time someone had given her anything with love and as they hurried to the stable, she grew light headed with excitement knowing this was going to be the first day of the rest of her life.

# Chapter 11

The sun beat down mercilessly cooking the spectators in their seats. Wild-eyed men filled with alcohol and a thirst for blood sat front and center, waiting for the tournament to begin. The women were no more decent, with their low cut bodices exposing nearly everything a proper lady would keep concealed, as they hooted and hollered, spilling warm ale all over the front of their clothing.

Jamie and Aldwin snuck in through the back entrance, avoiding this fiasco, following the red knight like lost puppies. He looked more regal than ever before with his brightly polished armor gleaming in the sunlight and the smell of sweet oil lofting in the air around his perfectly groomed hair. Even the scars on his face seemed less visible as he smiled and waved enthusiastically to the cheering crowd.

An elderly woman emerged from the gathering group of spectators that huddled under the thin tarp, stretched between long metal poles overhead. Her face was loose and hung in heavy folds that swallowed her pencil-like neck. At first glance she looked like a candle that was melting, with her swaying jowls and prunish complexion. But as she grew closer, her wax-like skin seemed to emanate a certain glow, a radiance that Jamie had never seen before. And as the old lady extended her liver-spotted hand, thick with green veins and cracked, bulging knuckles to give the knight a red rose, it suddenly dawned upon her that perhaps, true beauty came from within.

Actually Jamie had never thought about it before, beauty that is. Each time she looked in the mirror all she saw was her wild, chestnut hair and hollow, gray eyes staring back at her. Unlike other girls, she never gave a thought to make-up or a curling iron; it simply wasn't important. Surviving was, which meant that each waking moment was either dedicated to daydreaming to escape the hell in which she lived, or keeping her back flat against the wall to avoid any further assaults by the other girls.

But this older woman with her smile that shone brighter than a thousand suns gave her a moment of insight as the crowd jeered at her.

"You old crone," screeched a fat man in the back row, "You assault my eyes with your haggardly face! Be seated and let the games begin!"

"She's a certain one isn't she; with her swirly dress and lace bonnet?"

"Dressing up like you are one of them aren't you," chimed in a beggar woman with a tattered dress, "no use deary! We can see what you are!"

But the woman gave no mind to the wild insults of the surly group and accepted, with pink cheeks, a kiss on the hand by the red knight before sauntering back to her seat. She seemed so confident, so unbothered by all the chaos around her, ducking chunks of stale bread that were flung her way with a wink and a smile. And suddenly Jamie longed to be old, with flowing gray hair and weathered hands like this woman with a strength and wisdom that clearly came only with age. She seemed so vibrant and free and as she disappeared into the impatient mob, it made Jamie smile; giving her hope that someday she too would be that comfortable in her own skin.

The tournament began with a thunderous *boom* as each knight mounted their decorated horses and pranced around the small dirt arena, head erect, commanding the crowd's respect. Jamie peeked out from behind a dirty curtain in the knight's changing area, uncertain of what to do. Aldwin had fitted the knight with his armor and helped him mount his noble steed before arranging a pile of wooden lances near the curtain where Jamie stood. His posture was slightly tense as he crouched down by the lances, his fingers twitching in anticipation, arched just above the pile.

She wanted to help but didn't want to disturb him, so deep in concentration. Instead she studied him, knowing if something ever happened it would be her that would have to attend to these duties. A man with a thick, white mustache appeared atop a snow white stallion, prancing down the middle of the arena, kicking up dirt and small rocks. He wore no armor, only a black, pleated skirt and a matching jacket and on his head a small cap with a long, white plume. As soon as he entered a hush fell over the audience, leaving only the sound of his horse's hooves as they trotted back and forth, between the seated jousters.

"Is Lord Destrian at the ready?" he bellowed, pointing to the red knight. His helmet rattled as he nodded in response.

Jamie turned her attention towards the other man in armor, seated on a gray, speckled stallion. He looked confident, his shoulders back, his chest puffed out as his horse pawed the earth nervously. Both men were completely covered from head to toe, with nothing but thin slits cut in the helmets for them to see through. The other knight sported black colors with silver trim and looked quite impressive as the rays of the sun reflected off the shiny fabric.

"Then, if there are no further objections by either man, let the games begin!"

The crowd roared as both men backed their animals to their respective corners, waiting for the signal. A pretty young girl in a revealing dress walked by, enticing the audience to cheer louder for their jouster of choice. Sweat ran down Jamie's back, staining her new dress as she stood, trembling with anticipation. *I'm finally going to get to see a real joust!*

Brightly colored flags in red and black with silver trim were waved by boys at opposite ends of the field, signaling the start of the round. Aldwin tossed a wooden lance painted with red stripes up to Lord Destrian as a high pitched whistle pierced the air. With a might rush both knights spurred their horses forward, digging in their heels and lowering their heads as they poised for action. Each held a wooden spear pointed directly at the chest of the other man as they charge full speed ahead, never looking away.

*Oh my God, they're going to hit each other!* Jamie closed her eyes for a moment and turned her head, not wanting to see what was going to happen next. But curiosity overtook her and peeking out between her sweaty fingers she was witness to the exact moment when the tip of the lances collided with metal armor, showering the unprotected audience with sharp pieces of flying wood.

"Ouch! My arm!" shouted a skinny peasant in the front row as he pulled out a long sliver of wood from his bicep.

"My face, my beautiful face!" yelled a large woman in the middle section of the seating as she stood up and toddled away as fast as her stout little legs would carry her.

Jamie turned just in time to see the woman cover her face as blood spurted between her thick fingers. There was complete chaos in the crowd as everyone scrambled to see if they too had been struck by flying debris. Men shoved each other aside, swinging wildly if someone dared to get in their way. Women screamed and ran for the hills covering their faces and shielding their children with their bodies.

In the meantime, the jousters had dismounted and were duking it out on the ground. Both men had been dislodged by the simultaneous blow to chest and were now fighting for their lives amidst a cloud of dirt and animal manure. Jamie squinted to see what was going on, but the air was thick with dust making it hard to tell what was happening as the impassioned knights battled tirelessly. The master of ceremonies with the white mustache appeared, trotting his horse around the brainless duo, attempting to get them to stop.

"Enough I say! What sort of barbarity is this? Is this the behavior of a knight who answers to the king?"

Meanwhile the crowd had cleared out, leaving only a brave and curious few who wanted to see how it would all play out. Shaking her head in disbelief she looked to Aldwin to gage his reaction. *He must think this is crazy too!* To her shock and horror she saw him doubled over, lying face down on the ground.

"Aldwin! Aldwin!" There was no response.

Choking on dirt fumes Jamie leapt forward, falling hard when her foot hit an unseen rock in her path. Putting her arms out in front of her, she caught herself, scratching the palms of her hands on pieces of wood embedded in the dirt. A mace went flying over her head as she attempted to stand up, sticking fast to a nearby post. Crawling on her hands and knees she made her way over to her fallen companion.

"What's wrong? What happened?" He shook his head and turned away, not wanting her to see. But she was not so easily detoured.

Crawling around she faced him, pushing her face close to his stomach to see what was wrong. She gasped out loud as his fingers parted to reveal a long piece of wood sticking out of his stomach. Blood had soaked his new shirt and the stain was growing larger by the minute. Wrapping his arm around her neck she helped him up as they walked quickly towards the protective curtains in the back.

The fight between the knights was nearing an end as they had both lost their hand weapons in the fray. First the black and silver knight with his mace that went flying out of his hand and then Lord Destrian's sword that fell somewhere in the dust storm during their battle. The red knight had finally beaten his opponent into submission with his fists and as he towered over his quivering form, gasping from exhaustion, he removed his helmet so that he could look him straight in the eye. Drawing his sword the red knight placed the tip of it on his foe's throat, crushing his ribs with the heel of his heavy boot as he gloated over his defeat.

"Did you think yourself brave to stand against me here today, you **afterling** you son of a peasant?"

He sneered, barring his yellow teeth as his dark eyes glistened with evil delight. The knight in black and silver began to cough, spitting up mouthfuls of blood, choking on his own phlegm. But the red knight showed no mercy.

"Remove your helmet so that I may feast my eyes upon the man I am about to slay and so that you," he added haughtily, "may pay me proper respect!"

Slowly the fallen warrior removed his helmet, feeling the suction of sweat and blood that had accumulated during the fight tug at his skin as he pried it off and tossed it to the side. The red knight smiled as he leaned against the sword, watching the man underneath squirm as the blade began to slowly pierce his throat. Behind them, the master of ceremonies cried out for decency but his pleas fell on deaf ears.

"I should have killed you years ago when I first had the chance."

"Brother, please…." begged the man on the ground, raising his right hand in a sign of surrender, "think of our mother. How can her heart bear such news? First our father falls and now this?"

A hearty laugh emerged from the throat of the evil knight as he pushed the sword all the way through, pinning the man to the ground. Black blood came pouring out of the fallen warrior's throat as his body shook violently for a few moments before coming to rest forever. He stood back and watched as the life slipped from his brother, feeling a sense of calm wash over him. That little snake had always found a way to slither into their parents hearts, pushing him aside. All attention and praise was always lavished on him, the younger and more successful brother. But no more!

"Lord Destrian what manner of foul play is this? Not only do you slay a man in a friendly game that bears no real consequence on your life but show no mercy when it is revealed that man is of your same blood line?" The master of ceremonies shook his head as his black skirt fluttered in the gentle breeze.

But the red knight was undaunted and in a fit of rage, pulled his sword out of his brother's neck and pointed it straight at the old man's heart.

"I'll not be spoken down to by a man of your stature," he hissed, pressed the blade firmly against his unprotected skin, "this may be but a friendly game to you but it is my life! And I'll not have anyone interfering in it!"

And as the evil knight and the master of ceremonies argued, Jamie was tending to the wounds of her companion.

"Should we pull it out now?" She studied the wound extensively, removing his now ruined shirt and tossing it to the side. "It seems to have gone out through the top of your ribs."

His face pale, he shook his head in agreement. Gritting her teeth, Jamie grasped the wood and pulled it out slowly, feeling the body resist as he groaned in pain. Finally it came free, bringing with it blood and a clear, runny liquid she had never seen before. Reaching down next to her, she grabbed the discarded shirt and tore it into long strips, wrapping it around his slender waist in an attempt to stop the bleeding.

"We need some herb salve," he muttered, his eyes rolling around in his head.

"Herb salve? Well where is it?"

"Back at the—back at the—the house."

His breathing was labored as Aldwin struggled to maintain control. And then without warning he passed out, falling over like a sack of potatoes as his head bounced off the ground.

Jamie was growing desperate now and with no thought to her own safety ran into the midst of the verbal duel between the red knight and the old man, waving her arms frantically.

"He needs help, he's been hit," she yelled, stepping once again in front of the man who had wished to kill her for that very same act not so long ago.

He had removed his helmet and was staring down at her with those cold, soulless black eyes. There was no emotion in his voice when he spoke.

"Of what concern is that to me?"

Jamie was aghast. "It's of great concern to you! Without him, how are you going to get your armor off? I don't know how to do it! And how are you going to have all your horses ready on time? There are too many for me to do all by myself!"

He studied her for a moment, his eyes moving back and forth slowly between her and the master of ceremonies as if deciding which was more important. Finally he nodded and removed the tip of his sword from the old man's chest. Jamie watched as the men carried Aldwin away in the red knight's carriage. She was not invited to ride inside being a lowly servant, and so clung to the outside, praying that she would not fall off as it whisked its way back to the castle. And as the branches and twigs tugged at her hair and scratched her face, she felt tearless sobs begin to wrack her body. For the first time she was fearful of losing him. And the thought of facing that awful knight alone made her sick to her stomach.

*Dear God*, she prayed quietly as the carriage bounced over rocks and splashed across small fingers of running water, *don't let him die! Please! I promise to be nicer to him! I can't do this alone….*

# **Chapter 12**

The next few days passed by slowly giving Jamie ample time to think as she whiled away the hours brushing down sweaty animals and cleaning manure filled stalls. It was incredibly lonely without him and as she sat in the corner of the barn on top of a hard bag of feed, feeling the kernels dig into her backside, she began to worry. Since Aldwin was not with her, the morning ration of milk was gone along with the lunch time drop off.

She had no idea where he got the milk from considering there wasn't a cow in sight. And the red knight obviously thought she could fend for herself, or just didn't care about her eating in the afternoon. So all she had to sustain her was the water Aldwin had already drawn from the day before and left in the heated barn.

The first day went by rather smoothly as she pushed herself on an empty stomach, taking breaks throughout the day to maintain her strength. But by the end of the second day it was all she could do to keep from passing out as she labored in the unrelenting heat, feeling the acid gurgle in her stomach and tasting it again as she sat, fanning herself on the floor, chasing away the black spots that clouded her vision. Nights were no better as she shivered in the cold with no wood for the fire, wrapping herself in the thin blanket used for privacy and the sack cloth she had used when she first arrived.

By the start of the third day without him, Jamie began to grow desperate, dipping into the horse's food to feed her empty belly. It was gritty and tasted bitter but it was something. And after scarfing down a few fistfuls of dried grain she was ready to work. No sooner had she picked up a shovel then a thin, trembling shadow appeared at the opposite end of the barn. It moved slowly as if it were in pain, stopping several times to lean against the thick wooden beams, breathing heavily as it went.

It finally came to rest on a barrel of hay, tilting its head back and staring up towards the heavens. Jamie approached it carefully. Whoever it was lay completely hidden in shadow as the sun hid its face behind billowy white clouds. The first thing she recognized was the shoes, shiny and buff, a gift from the red knight for a job well done. His clothes were tattered, ruined by the massive amount of blood lost during the accident and the wooden shaft that pierced his stomach. But, he was alive.

A smile washed over her face as relief flooded her soul. *What luck!* He was trying to remain strong, turning his head as she approached; not wanting her to see the look of anguish that overcame him.

"I am glad you are okay."

He shook his head slowly in response, trying to move as little as possible. Jamie knew him well enough by now and understood that he didn't want to be catered to. He was a young boy, blossoming into a man and the thought of being fussed over by a girl didn't suit him.

"Water?"

She held out a cup of warm water but he shook his head no. He had been well cared for in the castle. Fresh, white bandages were wrapped around his torso and his face and hair looked freshly washed. He was too weak to work, but they had sent him out anyways; out in the heat with the back breaking labor that would break even the strongest of men after awhile. But he was determined. Pushing his way past her, he picked up a shovel and began to lift a heavy pile of manure into the wheel barrel.

The shovel made it up to his chest and as Jamie watched in horror, came clattering to the ground with Aldwin on top of it. She rushed over to him, shaking him with all her might. A weak moan escaped his throat as Jamie pulled out the shovel from underneath him, rolling him over on his back. His eyes rolled around like loose marbles and his tongue hung limply out of his mouth.

"Hey. Hey! Are you okay?"

He said nothing as the world spun in crazy circles around him, feeling her soft hands stroke his cheek before he blacked out completely. She was in a panic, not knowing what to do or who she could tell. Gently she lifted his head and laid it on a small stack of soft hay before running off to the castle. *There had to be someone there that could help. Maybe whoever had nursed him back to health was still there.*

A hollow thump rang in the air as her fist pounded hard against the enormous wooden door. Tilting her head back until it hurt, she tried in vain to see the top of the archway where the walkway and towers began. It seemed to reach into the heavens, as the tallest peaks touched the clouds, poking them into submission. After a few moments she banged on the door again, straining to hear any scurrying sounds of life from behind the double archway.

Pressing her ear against the door she heard what sounded like faint footsteps that tittered and tattered their way up to the door and hesitated for a moment before walking away quickly. Now, she was more irritated than ever, throwing her entire body against the doors, feeling the vibrations jolt through her torso as her shoulder slammed repeatedly against the impenetrable wood.

"Hey! Hey! I need help out here!"

She screamed at the top of her lungs until her throat was hoarse. And finally, after what seemed like an eternity, the large doors slowly creaked open to reveal a little old woman in a green dress with a matching hat and white scarf draped around her chin. She looked very nervous, peering out at Jamie from folds of thick skin, her eyes darting to and fro as she spoke.

"Yes, yes child what is it? That master of the house is very busy."

"I need help! Aldwin is hurt and he's lying in the stable and he can't move!"

The woman nodded quickly, fingering the panel with a trembling finger as she searched for the right response.

"They sent him back too soon. He's not better yet. He needs to heal!"

A soft smile broke across the woman's face, revealing a row of long, stained teeth. Squinting up at her she nodded once before ushering her inside. A cool gust of wind followed as the massive door slammed shut behind her, sending a chill down her spine. It reminded her of the cell in the pirate ship where she spent the majority of her time, almost losing her mind in the process.

But inside the castle was bright and cheery, filled with large paintings of accomplished men dressed in satin suits with noble dogs standing quietly at their sides. No one was smiling in these pictures and they all seemed to be staring at something off to the left that was visible only to them. A long table the length of the entire stable, covered with a thick, purple cloth and silver plates stood at the center of the room. Jamie walked towards it, mesmerized by the chairs that stood taller than her, covered with detailed carvings and heavy velvet backings.

But the old woman was in no mood for all this wandering around and grabbing her by the arm, led her into a smaller, more secluded room on the side. Large stained glass windows that ran from the ceiling to the floor, with brilliant hues of blue, red and yellow cast beams of colored light all around. Long, wooden benches with stiff backs and intricate designs stood in rows leading up to a high alter.

Sucking in a noisy breath Jamie moved towards the alter that stood high above the wooden benches at the front of the room. It had a long table covered in a delicate lace cloth that dripped off the sides, tickling the floor with its heavy tassels. There were three steps that led up to this table and on the either side sat large, jewel encrusted books held in place by swirling stands of oak. She had never seen jewelry on a book and as she moved closer, she reached out her hand to touch them as they glittered in the light of the stain glass.

A gentle smack brought her back to reality as the old woman stood before her, arms crossed, pointing towards a small bench in the back.

"You are to sit there. In the back is for the commoners. What would the master think if he came in and saw you standing up here?"

With a firm hand, the woman guided Jamie to a small, crudely cut bench in the very back, pushing down hard on her shoulders to make her sit.

"Now," she asked with a voice as sweet as honey, "what is it that I can do for you?"

# Chapter 13

The minutes ticked by slowly as Jamie sat in the secluded chapel, staring at illuminated stain glass windows, letting her eyes go in and out of focus on the many colors they displayed. Each piece of glass told a different religious story and as her eyes panned around the room she could almost follow along without need for interpretation. The first showed a mother and father kneeling over their baby in a barn. Everyone had a halo on their head, including the baby. There was a solemn reverence as they knelt with folded hands staring down at this child. The next showed a young boy in sandals and a white robe working with his father in a woodshop. Another showed that same young boy in front of a group of older men in a temple. He appeared to be showing them something as his arms were outstretched and the men sat, listening.

The last three seemed difficult to digest as that same young boy had grown tall; donning a full beard, still in sandals and a white robe was giving bread and fish to a large group of people. Jamie's head swiveled around the chapel to see what would happen next, following the brightly colored panels with intensity. Now that same man was stretched out on a cross with nails in his hands, stripped of his clothing, as a gathering crowd stood below, watching. The final panel showed the man standing in front of a tomb with beams of light shooting out from his body as a woman knelt at his feet, weeping.

It was all very strange to her and as she pondered the meaning a loud creek followed by a swishing sound gave distraction, as the same old woman in the green dress entered the room once more. She seemed more flustered than before, looking around as if she were expecting the boogey man to come jumping out from behind one of the decorated benches. Clicking her tongue against the roof of her mouth, she motioned for Jamie to stand up and follow her.

Reluctantly Jamie agreed, not wanting to leave this sanctuary. It seemed so peaceful and beautiful. *How could Aldwin say there were bad things in here?* She just couldn't imagine.

Out the heavy wooden door with brightly polished gold handles and from under the archway they emerged, back into the dining room. Everything seemed more alive, as women in plain cotton dressed with aprons tied around their thick waists scurried about, carrying large, silver dishes on their shoulders. It was lunch time for the master of the house and Jamie was curious to see what he ate, especially since they were given such meager scraps on which to survive. But the woman had no time for her to stop and observe as she kept her hands firmly on her shoulders, steering her towards the castle door.

"The master will be home soon. Out with you now." She said, giving her a gentle shove towards the enormous doors. But Jamie would not be put off.

"What about Aldiwn? Is he okay? Did you get him help?"

"He will be fine child, now, out with you."

The blood began to pound in Jamie's ears as the woman, surprisingly strong for her age, attempted to force her out. She was not going to let this happen. They may have been servants to the red knight but that didn't mean she was going to let her partner die because of his inferior status. Ducking under the woman's stiff arms, she jumped behind her, forcing her to turn around and face her.

"I'm not leaving until you get him help. He's my friend and I'm not going to let him die!"

The old woman's mouth began to soften around the corners as the flabby, pale flesh sunk into the folds like warm play dough. At first Jamie was afraid she was going to be angry, but as she studied the face of this well dressed stranger, there was a twinkle in her eyes that gave way to the true magic underneath those restrictive clothes and that no nonsense voice.

"We have already retrieved him. His agrum[12] has already gone down. He will be fine." She added, patting her shoulder as she walked her to the door.

The rest of the day went by quickly with no thought to food or rest as she worked tirelessly brushing down each animal and laying fresh hay in their stalls. She didn't know how much longer Aldwin would need to heal. But as she crunched down on some stale horse feed she had put in her pockets that evening, she decided she would just have to endure it. He was clearly too weak to work and trying to force him to come back too soon would only make things worse.

Two more days passed and still no sign of her companion. The moon was growing fuller as she had spent many cold, sleepless nights observing it through the cracked windows in the

---

[12] *swelling of the cheeks*

**cruck.** It seemed like this whole journey was just bad timing as the one person who she communicated with was missing from the picture. But she pressed on, cleaning and scrubbing and stacking the hay bales in the corner since she did not possess the strength to lift them by herself.

Then finally, as she sat in the corner that blistering hot afternoon, feeling the beads of sweat drip off the end of her nose, draining her of all life she saw him. He seemed taller than before, standing erect in the doorway, his shoulders stretching almost the entire length of the opening. Well rested with new clothes and a head full of clean, wavy hair he was back. Smiling broadly, he walked over and sat next to her, producing a turkey leg from a wrapped cloth behind his back. Hungrily Jamie gorged on the greasy meat, jerking her head down in acknowledgement, her eyes fixed on the prize.

When she had finished she stared up at him, grateful and exhausted. He was alive, coming back to help her with the heavy work load. Everything was exactly as it should be.

"It seems you have fared well without me."

Jamie snorted in response. "Not really. I've had to eat horse food just to stay alive and the cabin is freezing at night."

He nodded sympathetically, wrapping his arm around her shoulder and giving her a tight squeeze. The air seemed to shift as they sat in silence, staring into each other's eyes. She needed him, of that there was no doubt. But for the first time in his life, Aldwin felt like he needed someone too. He had been at it alone for so long he had forgotten what that felt like. When they were together, the work load didn't seem so heavy and the freezing nights in a rundown shack didn't feel quite so awful with someone to keep you company.

They worked in unison, sweeping, scrubbing and hauling for the rest of the day, never saying a word. Things were back to normal and the knot in Jamie's stomach had finally dissolved. All the worry and fear about his survival and her ability to maintain on her own was gone.

That evening he had a special surprise for her, producing yet another hunk of meat and some warm potatoes for their supper. They ate quietly by the roaring fire and even as she chewed a smile could be seen on her face. For the first time in a long time, she was happy. But the night of enchantment didn't end there. When they had finished Aldwin led her out to the barn wrapped in a blanket, to a young pony that stood waiting, stomping the ground impatiently; saddled and ready to go.

She squealed with delight as they rode at full speed into the darkened forest. Wrapping her arms around his firm stomach and resting her head on his back, she leaned in to him, feeling the rhythm of the powerful animal that almost rocked her to sleep. When they reached the clearing they dismounted as before, taking off their shoes to feel the velvety soft grass tickle their tired toes. But this time something was different. There were burn marks all over the grass and the smell of burnt meat lingered in the air.

"Did someone come here to cook something?" She just couldn't imagine.

Aldwin kept silent, pointing to a glowing red cloud on the far side of the forest. It seemed to hover and dance in the air as if it were bewitched, twisting and curling into strange shapes as it tangled with the leaves overhead. As if in a daze she followed it, her eyes fixed on this strange cloud of light. Aldwin called after her, but she didn't seem to hear him as she moved deeper into the forest.

Her legs burned from hours of hard labor but she pushed herself, determined to see where this mysterious smoke was coming from. And just when she thought she couldn't walk another step they found it. There, in the middle of woods with a crumbling chimney and lopsided windows stood the strangest looking cabin they had ever seen. Even the door seemed sideways, as everything was tilted to the left making them feel off balance the longer they looked at it.

Timidly she approached the house, inspecting it from every angle. Aldwin stood back, holding the tired horse by the reins, ready to jump in and save her at a moment's notice. Even the wood on the walls seemed odd, curling and twisting off the house like it was a tree sprouting roots. And as Jamie tried to move around to the back of the house she realized it was built into something tall and hard but with the lack of light she couldn't see what it was.

Suddenly, the door flew open and a stream yellow light pierced the darkness. Jamie jumped back as a hooded figure hovered in the doorway. He was small in stature and carried a long, twisted cane. After several moments of nothingness he finally spoke.

"Eh! So, you've finally come to see me? About time!" He added before shuffling back into the protective confines of his house.

The door remained open, leaving a trail of glowing uncertainty on the grass before them. Aldwin stood frozen on the opposite side of the bar of light, looking first at Jamie and then at the house. A strange tingling sensation was in the air almost as if the hooded figure by somehow opening his door had opened up the magic of the forest. With their eyes slowly adjusting to this newfound source of light, it became obvious why this house had seemed so strange.

The front seemed fairly normal aside from the crooked windows and cockeyed door, but as they looked towards the back and around the sides they noticed it was built into the base of a large tree. Never had they seen such a sight as the massive roots curled up and around the sides of the cabin, making large archways all around. The tree itself seemed to reach into the heavens with a thick trunk and long branches that scratched the stars. A few of the branches hung low to the ground, covered in a shiny green moss that dangled over the doorway.

It was more magical than anything Jamie could have ever imagined. And as she took a few steps forward she noticed large toadstools that reached her waist, growing out of the ground. They looked like tables or perhaps umbrellas for the frogs and other small critters of the woods, with their shiny mushroom heads glistening in the moonlight.

The smell of freshly baked bread poured out of the open doorway, filling her nostrils as she stumbled forward for a closer look. Aldwin whispered out a warning behind her. He knew better than to go traipsing into a stranger's home. But Jamie ignored him. There seemed to be something all too familiar about this crumpled figure that stood in shadow, beckoning them with bony, liver spotted hands. And as she walked timidly into this unknown place, squinting from the intensity of the yellow beam, she intended to find out what.

# **Chapter 14**

The moon hung low in the sky, making every shadow appear more menacing as branches raked their angry fingers against the stone walls of the castle. He couldn't sleep the red devil. At first it was too hot and as he bellowed for his servants to come and open all the windows, two small figures hidden under the blanket of night stole away past his window. Rubbing his eyes he jumped away, fearful that he had seen a ghost. And after killing his brother it was easy to see why.

Taking a step back he shook his head vigorously, clearing all sense of sleep and doubt from his mind before going back to the window. The two figures were sitting, huddled on top of an animal, riding at full speed, and as they disappeared into the woods he silently vowed to find out who they were and what they were up to. At that moment a young boy entered the room dressed in rags with a candle grasped in his trembling hand. He wore no shoes and as he rubbed the sleep from his bloodshot eyes, he found himself cornered in the back of the bedroom as the lord of the manor hovered over him with clenched fists making him a wicked proposition.

Meanwhile, Jamie had made her way into the old man's tree home, shielding her hazel eyes from the fierce light as large, black spots appeared in her vision. She was use to the shade of the barn and the light of the moon and this neon beam seemed very unnatural, searing her corneas as she pushed forward. Aldwin stood in the doorway, ready to run or reach in and grab her, whatever the case may be. His eyes were downcast as he too fought against the swords of brightness that radiated from the tiny room.

"Come in, come in children and sit down." His voice was gravely but soothing.

"It's—it's too bright," Jamie wined, knocking her kneecap into a low-backed chair, "we can't see!"

Not a word was spoken but moments later the room went from a gaudy brightness to pitch dark. She couldn't even see her hand in front of her face and as her eyes searched for the familiar light of the moon through the open door, it slammed shut rattling the entire house. Jamie felt a chill inch its way up her spine as she knew there was no one on the other side of the door.

Aldwin was shoved forward when the door closed, sending him reeling into the table, knocking the wind out of him as the edge of the wood dug deep into his stomach.

Jamie heard him gasp as he was thrown forward and as she reached for him, she palmed her way through the blackness grasping the edge of the table for support. But suddenly a flickering flame in the far corner of the room caught her attention for this was no ordinary light. It looked like the wick of a candle had been lit but the fire, as it danced and dipped through the air, was not attached to anything.

She reached Aldwin, feeling his strong arms grab and pull her slowly to the ground with him. There, they watched this enchanted flame as it swirled around the table, past the fireplace and finally coming to rest in the hand of the old man who stood, waiting with an unlit candle clenched in his fist. The light burned tall and bright, nearly reaching the roof, illuminating the room as the stranger whispered words of encouragement.

"There, there," he cooed, gently stroking the flame with his finger, "just relax you've almost got it now."

The spit of fire jumped higher at first, tickling the top of ceiling making Jamie gasp in fright. *What if it set the house on fire? We would all die, burnt to a crisp since the whole place is made of wood!* But soon it lowered itself, coming to rest neatly on the burnt wick of the white candle in the man's withered hand. It was like a small child, being coaxed into submission. Jamie breathed a sigh of relief as she and Aldwin stumbled to their feet.

"What kind of a candle is THAT?" She wondered aloud, staring intently at the dancing sprite.

Aldwin squeezed her arm, letting her know that some questions should not be asked. The old man smiled broadly, revealing several missing teeth as his blue eyes darted mischievously around the room. His face was still guarded by the darkness as one candle could hardly be thought to light an entire room.

As if he was reading her mind the stranger raised his hands and mumbled some words under his breath. A warm wind swept through the room, stinging her eyes and cheeks as she struggled to see what was going on. The sound of pages flipping open and wooden utensils being flung across the table echoed in her ears as she clung desperately to Aldwin, determined not to get swept away.

"What are you doing old man?" He asked, trying to make sense of the situation.

But his words were swept away with the wind as it blew from one corner of the room to the other, whipping their hair around their confused faces. The bewitched flame that was sitting so respectfully in the stranger's hand, suddenly leapt around the room, bowing gracefully, as it stopped in several places along the walls. Jamie tried to follow it with her eyes but found it difficult as it waivered from statuesque and vibrant to a quivering spark that threatened to go out completely.

A low rumbled emerged from the man's throat as his arms began to shake, extended high above his head. Jamie buried her head in Aldwin's chest as the room hummed with an intensity that she had never felt before. It didn't feel threatening and as they stood, huddled together between the fireplace and the rough, wooden table, a sense of calm began to wash over her. A giggle worked its way up from her belly and got caught in her throat as the warm air swirled around them. Unusual as it was it didn't seem appropriate to laugh.

The old man let out a long, guttural moan, waggling his bony fingers towards the sky as the rogue flame returned to him, settling on top of the candle he held, almost as if it had never left. His head dropped and as soon as his chin touched his chest, the room was ignited with a soft, white glow. Jamie picked her head up to see a ring of candles that stretched around the entire room, all lit with tiny tongues of fire. But instead of being red, or orange like most flames, they produced an angelic, white light that seemed to envelope her like snow on Christmas morning.

Miss Legree was not fond of letting the girls go outside in the winter. She feared they would get frostbite, or slip and fall on the icy metal bars of the playground. But one wonderful Christmas morning she relented after hearing the many pleas of the bored young girls.

"Oh Miss Legree, can't we go outside, just for a few minutes?"

"Yeah," chimed in the one with curly red hair, "it's so dull in here!"

"And look at all the fun they're having!" wined another as she pointed enviously at the neighboring children who were outside in their winter gear, tossing snowballs at each other and giggling furiously.

Bowing her head the headmistress finally gave in.

"All right girls," she said gently, wrapping them in as much clothing as possible, "stay on the sidewalk out front where I can see you."

They didn't have proper winter clothes. Those cost money something the orphanage didn't have. So they delved through a box of hand-me-down clothes donated by the local charity and bundled up the best they could. It was quite a sight to behold as they emerged from the girl's home wrapped in four shirts of varying sizes and three pairs of mismatched socks to warm their feet. Gleefully, the danced under the falling snowflakes, sticking out their tongues and squealing with delight whenever they caught one.

A white truck pulled up in front of the orphanage and a man in a brown suit and overcoat dropped off several large packages at their door. Everyone gathered around to see what he had brought, sticking in their tiny fingers, poking at what was inside. But the headmistress took control of the situation, carefully opening each package as the beginnings of a smile crossed her shriveled face.

"It seems," she said, her thin lips puckering with emotion, "that the charity has been most generous this year." All the girls gathered around to listen. "They have not only donated the extra clothes but," she paused for dramatic effect, "four sleds and extra mittens to boot!"

The girls cheered enthusiastically, shoving each other aside in order to get a closer look. Miss Legree pulled each one out of the box with care, wiping it down before setting it gingerly on the snow covered ground. Several hands grabbed at it, stroking the smooth wooden surface, feeling the sharp sting of the cold, metal runners underneath.

"Can we ride these down the hill?" asked one girl with piercing blue eyes.

Everyone else joined in, begging for a change to ride it down the small slope just over the hill. With a reluctant sigh Miss Legree nodded, assigning one sled to each girl she felt was the most responsible.

"Lisa, you take that one," she said, motioning towards a doe—eyed burnet with long, straight hair, "and Maria you take this one. Janie and Jesse, you take the last two. Now," she said in her oh so responsible voice, "you children be careful. I'll be there to keep an eye on you, but no pushing and no shoving. Just because it is Christmas does not mean we should not conduct ourselves as young ladies."

Everyone groaned rolling their eyes as their frozen fingers twitched with excitement.

"And remember," she called out as they ran off with the sleds, "everyone gets a turn."

Excitement filled the air as the girls made their way up the small, snow covered hill. Some fell down and made snow angels others held hands as they helped each other up to the top. Jamie was by herself in the back of the group but even now the happiness seemed to fill the air around her, giving her new hope. Patiently she waited her turn, watching as the other girls yelled at the top of their lungs as they flew down the hill, coming to a stop just before a small patch of woods at the bottom.

It looked like great fun and even though the slope was rather small, Jamie was looking forward to her turn. Some of the girls went in pairs, gripping each other for dear life as they screamed in unison, getting a mouthful of snow for their trouble. Finally, it was her turn and as the last girl walked back up the hill with the sled she could feel a tingling sensation in her fingertips. *At last!* But the girl walked right past her, handing the shiny, snow covered sled to the person behind her.

"Hey! What gives?" She had been waiting for so long and now to have this happen.

"Ignore her," the curly haired blond said to the confused girl who was now holding the sled, "SHE doesn't get a turn."

"Oh yes I do!" There was no way she was going down without a fight.

"Oh yeah?"

"Yeah!"

Jamie reached out and grabbed the sled from the dumbfounded girl behind her. But the blond stepped in front of her and pulled back, her blue eyes on fire. A tugging match ensued to which Jamie lost when two other girls stepped in to help their friend. Her hands stung as the sled was ripped out of her hands, raking against the sharp metal poles on the bottom.

"I told you, you don't get a turn!"

A small crowd had gathered to watch this display and were laughing uncontrollably as Jamie stood there with bloody hands, her mouth open. *What had just happened?*

"Why don't you go sit over there," the girl said, motioning to the trees behind the hill, before turning her back on Jamie.

With clenched fists that leaked blood she left, moving towards the small forest. It was not that she wanted to obey this bully, but the trees were the one place where she felt safe. And as she settled down between two towering giants with thick needles that scratched her cheek she closed her eyes and allowed her imagination to carry her away, as the girls zoomed down the slope, laughing all the while.

"We need to get out of here." Aldwin whispered in her ear, pulling on her sleeve as he moved towards the door.

He was rattled but wouldn't admit it. The old man turned to face them, his long hood falling to the tip of his nose. Slowly, he moved towards them, his hands hidden under the thick folds of the robe.

"Let us go," his voice was calm but there was fear in his eyes as he spoke, "we have done you no harm."

"Nor have I done any to you, young man."

Jamie smiled in spite of herself, stepping forward to face this hooded stranger. "My name is Jamie and this," she said motioning towards the reluctant figure behind her, "is Aldwin."

A low clucking sound escaped the man's throat as he thought this over. "Mine is Dobromil, pleased to make your acquaintance."

"We really must be going," Aldwin said, inching his way towards the door, "the sun rise…"

The old man nodded as if he understood and without another word, waved his hand at the door which flung itself open, making a great swooshing sound as the night air blew in. Aldwin pulled Jamie outside and towards their grazing horse as the old man's voice carried on the wind.

"Come back and see me again soon!"

They rode back to the castle in silence as Jamie contemplated all the wondrous things she had witnessed. It would be great work convincing Aldwin that they should return to visit the old man in the woods. But as they their breathing fell in line with the rhythm of the horse, and she felt the muscles tense and relax in his back as he steered them home, she knew it could be done.

# Chapter 15

Two days had passed since their visit with the old man in the forest and there was nothing else Jamie could think of. Never had she witnessed such magic and as she hummed an off—key tune while brushing down one of the horses, a soft smile claimed her face. Aldwin noticed there was something different about her. Before, she used to have to be dragged out of bed with threats of being beaten by the red knight and the lure of warm milk. Now, she rose before him, twirling around on her tip toes as she swept the floor with a makeshift broom like a princess at a royal ball.

"What's so funny?" He was determined to discover the reason for this sudden change.

"Huh?"

She heard him and yet she didn't as her eyes glossed over, thinking about the enchanted little tree house with the dancing candle flames and the strange old man who possessed such mysterious powers.

"You have been distracted all day and look," he said, motioning to the bucket beside her, "you forgot to add the soap. You scrubbed down this animal with nothing but water."

For a moment she froze, uncertain of how to react. It had been another long, hard day with little more than scraps to keep them alive and the blazing sun their constant companion. This mistake would cost her time, valuable time, as she would now have to redo the entire bath.

Lowering her head, she squinted, furrowing her brow as she contemplated this. Aldwin moved around the horse and put his arm around her shoulders, ready to console her. A gasp escaped her throat as Jamie turned her head. He could feel the shaking of her torso as she looked away, too ashamed to cry in front of him.

But a gleeful yelp caught his attention and as she slowly pulled away he realized, that she was laughing! Girlish giggles snuck out from between clenched lips as she did her best to hide her hilarity. And as her body crumpled to the floor she could conceal it no longer and gave herself over to the laughter, tossing her head back to the ceiling and *whooping* so loudly it began to frighten the horses.

Aldwin didn't quite know what to make of it as he stood there, watching this sad, morose young girl indulge herself in a moment of sheer happiness. Finally, the giggling died down and as Jamie lay in a puddle of dirty horse water, gasping for breath, he decided to take her back. It was no coincidence that her mood changed after their encounter in the woods and if it meant making her happy, he would do it. It was three days until they celebrated the resting period when they wouldn't have to get up and go to work the next morning; but Aldwin decided he could not wait. And judging by the looks of it as she struggled to sit up, her body, limp from laughter, neither could she.

And when the moon was out, shining in all its glory, they stole away, quiet as mice into the woods. But this time they were not alone. Careful as he was, Aldwin failed to notice a skinny shadow, keeping close to the ground that slinked along, following a few steps behind.

He had been living in the castle only a short while and although his bed was in the basement with the rats he considered himself lucky. The rest of his family had been wiped out by a plague and as the only living male remaining; it was his job to secure hearth and home for himself and a possible future bride. What he was doing was wrong, spying on these poor, unsuspecting servants. And oh, what a beating they would receive when he reported back to the red knight, telling him of all the scandalous things he did see.

But as he ran alongside their horse, listening to them laugh merrily, he knew it was either them, or him. If he did not give an account of all that occurred it would be him that was beaten, starved and thrown to the wolves; literally. Rumor had it, the red knight kept a pen of wolves behind the castle that he fed all his unruly servants to. Shuddering at the thought he pushed himself onwards, his bird—like legs pumping furiously to keep up as the horse began to canter through the dark trees.

They returned to the same place they had before, just beyond the open circle in the center of the woods with the smell of baked bread in the air. Aldwin dismounted first and with a quick swing, Jamie was helped to the ground, removing her shoes and letting the cool grass tickle the pads of her feet. She waited patiently while her companion walked around, studying the trees and measuring the distance of the moon.

"It's not here." His voice came quietly, as he moved around, darting in and out of the bushes, searching.

"Not here?" She wondered aloud. *How could that be possible?* "Are you sure we're in the right place?"

"Yes."

She shook her head in disgust, turning to pat the velvety nose of the horse beside her. *There must be some mistake. After all, houses just don't get up and walk away, do they?* But maybe this one did. Minutes seemed like hours and after awhile Aldwin was ready to call it a night.

"It has just," his words trailed off as he scratched his head in disbelief, "vanished!"

A sinking feeling filled the pit of Jamie's stomach. She had been waiting for this, thinking of nothing else and now, only to be turned away. *Well I won't accept it!*

"But he said," she insisted, her bottom lip quivering, "He said that we should come back!"

"Well, that's just the thing with magic men. They are never what they seem and never to be trusted. Let that be a lesson to you."

Jamie nodded, lowering her head to hide her disappointment as Aldwin walked over to take the horse. All of a sudden there was a blinding flash of light and before them stood the hooded figure, arms crossed, drumming his bony fingers on his chest. He seemed irritated as he stood, shoulders hunched, with blue eyes that burned from within the darkness of the robe. Aldwin walked over and grabbed the horse's reigns as Jamie stood, open mouthed at this phenomenon before them.

"Ah," he said in a gravelly voice, "I've been waiting for you."

Turning on his heel, the stranger disappeared into the trees, leaving the two of them scrambling in hot pursuit. They followed him for what seemed like a great distance, crossing several babbling brooks and dodging large mosquitoes that buzzed loudly in their ears. And after what seemed like an eternity they happened upon the same titled house with the table sized toadstools built into a mighty oak.

Relief washed over Jamie as she stumbled through the door, leaving Aldwin to tend to the horse. The first thing she did was flop down at the table, propping her head up on her hands. She was exhausted and as her stable companion entered, his face streaked with sweat and his eyes glassy from lack of sleep, she began to wonder if they should have come out here at all.

"Come, sit by the fire children. I will fetch you some Adam's Ale[13] and we can talk."

It took Jamie a moment to stand up and walk over to where Aldwin was sitting as she had just gotten so comfortable at the table. Her eyelids drooped as she leaned against him, watching the flames dance and crackle before her. A huge yawn escaped her as she studied the oranges, yellows and hints of blue that paraded before her. It seemed just like the fire they had at home in the little **cruck** that the wind whistled through, causing them many cold, sleepless nights.

A shiny mug was shoved into her tired hands and as the lukewarm water tickled her tonsils a strange feeling began to come over her. It was as if she was floating high, over the trees like a bird, her arms out straight, head erect as she scanned the ground below. There were many people on the ground, toiling in the hot sun that she somehow did not feel. They looked like ants dressed in peasant clothes and as she flew forward, into the deep, blue sky the world went dark.

She awoke several hours later not knowing where she was. It took her a moment as she lay absolutely still, fearful if she moved she would fall, patting the floor around her with trembling fingertips. Aldwin sat up a few moments later, his eyes wild as he looked around the room. The sun had just started to peek over the hills, its warm fingers pushing through the cracks in the wall, signaling they were not too late.

The rest of the day was a blur as they went through the motions, never conscience of their surroundings. Lunch came and went and as they sat, chewing on hard jerky, the colors of the hay and the floorboards going in and out of focus they wondered just what had happened. To Jamie it felt like it had all been a very strange dream and when thinking about it in the light of day,

---

[13] *water*

seemed ridiculous. But she had learned with the pirates just how strange reality became once she chose to embark on an adventure in the museum.

Unfortunately things did not turn out so magical for the young boy who was sent to follow them. Fearful that the red knight would skin him alive for failing to bring back any relevant information he fled on foot, over the hills never to be heard from again. How could he explain what he saw when he wasn't even sure what it was? The only thing he could remember was following someone or something into the forest and then it was like his memory had been wiped clean. Men were burned as witches for speaking in such a manner. And as he disappeared over the horizon leaving a trail of urine and shame behind him, the trees in the forest seemed to breathe a sigh of relief, as the leaves spoke like tiny tongues, whispering on the wind, *children you are safe now, you are safe.*

# **Chapter 16**

"So good to see you again children; enter, enter, you are always welcome in my home!"

He spoke with great enthusiasm as he motioned for them to step inside the tree house. It had taken a great deal of convincing to get Aldwin to return to the forest. He was certain there was witchcraft afoot after what happened last time.

"Look, if we don't go back we'll never know what really happened."

They had gone another whole day without speaking of what had occurred, mainly because they were not sure what had. Aldwin would have been perfectly happy to avoid the subject completely and never go back again. But Jamie was relentless.

"We know that man is a witch. If we are caught speaking with him, we will be burned as sympathizers to the cause."

"No he's not! He is a good person, I can tell."

Jamie had no idea what a witch really was. They never spoke of them at the orphanage. In fact Miss Legree took great precautions not to mention anything that would be upsetting to the younger inhabitants. But she would defend this stranger against what was an obvious attack on his character, as she felt he had something to teach them. He intrigued her, living out all alone in the woods in a house that seemed to move as if by magic. Aldwin shook his head *no*.

"Look," she said, throwing down the heavy pitchfork, showering him with loose hay, "if he was really bad then he would have hurt us by now. We were asleep last time. That would have been his chance to really do something bad. But instead we woke up in our own beds and the horse was safely back in the barn!"

He was listening intently even though he pretended to ignore her and turn his back as he flung dirty hay out of the stall door.

"Well," Jamie said, picking up her fork once again, "I'm going back with or without you. I know the forest by now and how to ride well enough."

And low and behold there they were, standing in the old man's kitchen once again. She could always convince him—so stubborn and determined to have her own way. Little did Jamie realize that was soon going to cost her more than she bargained for. But at the moment all they could do was bask in the white glow of the enchanted house, watching as the hooded figure scurried about dusting off chairs and tabletops. Great clouds of dust filled the air as they choked on the fumes of filth that oddly enough didn't seem to be there two days ago.

"Forgive me," he mumbled, waving his withered hands in the air as he attempted to clean, "it is difficult to keep a clean house for an old man like me."

And through the puffs of dirt, Jamie saw him walk to the center of the room, close his eyes and take a deep breath. But this was no ordinary breath. As soon as he began to inhale, the sooty air began to swirl around their heads, sounding like a wind storm in the desert. And what were once clouds of dust turned into swirling tornado tunnels that tore around the room with lightening speed.

Jamie screamed and buried her head in Aldwin's shoulder as the warm air blew viciously around her dress, scratching her legs with the hard grains of dirt and bread that fell from the table. Unable to help herself she peeked through clenched hands as the old stranger titled his head back until his nose pointed towards the ceiling and took in a noisy breath. Suddenly the dust tornados fell into place, surrounding the man like a street gang. Then one by one they leapt from the floor and into his nostrils, disappearing quicker than when they came.

They stood, speechless, staring at this unknown magician who took the opportunity to daintily take a handkerchief from one of his sleeves and pat the end of his nose. A smile broke across Jamie's face as the old man sneezed and a little puff of dirt came out of his nose like a fire breathing dragon. Turning his chin up slightly, the man smiled back, revealing a row of white teeth and sparkling blue eyes, before lowering his gaze once more.

Aldwin's grip on her was painful as he stared intently at the stranger, his eyes burning with distrust.

"Ah, that's better," the man said, walking over to the fireplace, "and now what can I get you to drink?"

"No," Aldwin said, stepping bodily in front of Jamie.

"But you must be thirsty, after such a long trip." His back was to them as he fumbled for a set of glasses in a tiny, overhead cabinet.

"I said no."

He didn't shout. He didn't have to. His voice rang with authority. And even at sixteen years old he was a man, forged in the fires of heavy labor and self—reliance. It made Jamie proud to see him act this way but also irritated as she desperately wanted to forge a relationship with this new and very interesting person.

"Well what about you, young lady? Would you like something?"

The air in the room grew heavy as Aldwin inched closer to the stranger, his fists clenched tightly at his side. A low clucking sound emerged from the old man's throat as he continued to face the cabinets, seemingly unaware of the growing storm behind him. Finally he produced two silver mugs to which he clung tightly as he placed them gently on the counter in front of him.

"You need not fear me boy. I am not your enemy."

His voice was soft and reassuring and seemed to lighten the mood as he turned to face her angry stable companion, mugs in hand. Aldwin let the old man place the cups on the table in front of them but refused to allow them to drink anything. The air was quiet as Aldwin stared at the hooded figure, rapping his fingers loudly against the wooden table. Jamie was beginning to feel wildly uncomfortable and decided to break the ice. Slowly her hand snaked towards the cup. But an angry smack against the back of her hand was a painful reminder of who was really in charge. He would not allow it, not after what happened last time.

"She can drink and so can you. There is nothing in there that will harm you."

"Lies!" He spat the word at the stranger like a snake spewing venom.

The hooded figure did not move his face in shadow and his back to the fireplace. Liver spotted hands emerged from the flowing sleeves and began to tap together in front of his chest. A low chuckle escaped his throat as he nodded sympathetically in their direction.

"What happened last time was for your own protection."

"So you admit that you poisoned us!" Aldwin was nearly foaming at the mouth as he said this.

"Not poisoned, drugged."

"You crazy old fool!"

And with an impressive show of strength he grabbed Jamie by the arm and pulled her over the chair and onto the floor in front of him. For a moment she was airborne and dreadfully afraid of what would happen next. But as her feet hit the floor and strong fingers pushed against her back, guiding her towards the door, that sinking feeling of defeat hit her.

"There was someone following you from the red knight's castle that would have unveiled your little secret. I merely intervened on your behalf."

Jamie stopped dead in her tracks, pulling away from her friend with all her strength as she turned around and faced the mysterious stranger.

"What exactly did you do?"

Curiosity was one of her downfalls, always seeming to get her into some sort of trouble. Like the time Miss Legree, the headmistress of the orphanage told them the story about a very special box she kept at the foot of her bed in her room. Normally stories like this would dull Jamie to tears but when the old crone mentioned the words *hope chest*, her boredom turned into intrigue as the woman went into great detail about how each girl should have one and what should be kept inside.

"A hope chest is something every girl should own. It holds precious keepsakes that we would want to use when we are married. Now," she said with emotional gusto, "does anybody have an idea of what some of those things might be?"

Silence fell in the room until the curly—headed blond in the front row spoke.

"I think," she said in her prissiest voice, "that a cooking recipe might be one."

"Excellent! Yes! Everyone knows that a good wife must know how to cook for her husband. Anyone else?"

"A wedding dress?"

"Some silverware?"

"A book about being a good mommy?"

The list went on and on but as Jamie's eyes glazed over her mind began to wander about what Miss Legree kept in her hope chest. She couldn't imagine this dried up old prune having ever wanted to be married. And later that afternoon while everyone else was outside during recess, Jamie snuck back into the orphanage and stole away up to the old bat's room.

The door was locked, but after a few swift kicks it flung open, revealing a place that time forgot with lace and cobwebs covering every inch of available space. It seemed cold and creepy and as she made her way over to the large wooden chest at the foot of the bed, her heart beat quickened. The floorboards creaked alarmingly as she stood in front of the plain box, yanking on the lid that seemed to be nailed shut.

"Well, two can play at this game," she shouted aloud as she bent down and began to violently shake the chest from side to side.

After a few minutes she grew tired of wrestling with the box and reached into her pocket and pulled out a butter knife she had borrowed from the kitchen for just such an occasion. Skillfully, she slid the knife between the lid and the base and twisted and pushed down, grunting with all her might. And at long last, success, as the lid flew open and a big cloud of dust filled her nostrils.

Waving her hand in front of her face, Jamie managed to clear the air enough to put her head down and see what was inside. And what she saw astounded her. Inside the hope chest there was a blue cardboard box filled with old pictures of Miss Legree. The only reason Jamie could tell it was her was because of the faint, swirly penmanship on the bottom that said: *Abigail Legree and suitor*.

It shocked her to see a young, fresh faced girl with long brown hair and sparkling eyes holding a croquet mallet in the middle of large field. Behind her stood a young man about the same age, handsome in face with kind eyes. He had his arms wrapped around Miss Legree and both of them were laughing hysterically at something Jamie could not see. What stunned her most about the picture, besides the fact she never thought Miss Legree was ever young, was the look of genuine happiness on her face.

There were more pictures of her and that same young man on a boat, wearing their Sunday best and smiling broadly at the camera in a series of various poses. And then, at the bottom of the cardboard box, were some old, cracked photos of Miss Legree when she first arrived at the orphanage. At the bottom of the picture it said: *My first job at the all girl's home.*

But these pictures were different than the others. There was no handsome young man in a suit and tie behind her, making her laugh. And the long hair that once hung free was tied up in the same tight bun she wore now. Gone was her flowy summer dress and it its place, the long, black dress of doom Miss Legree donned to this day. And as Jamie studied the picture she realized that more than her appearance had changed. Although the woman's face was smiling in the picture, the light in her eyes was gone.

And later that day as Jamie scrubbed the dining room floor as punishment for her sins, she contemplated what she had seen. *What happened to that young, free spirited girl in the previous pictures? Why did she not marry the young man? Did he leave her? And why?* And most importantly, *what made her stop trying to be happy?*

"Let's just say I made it difficult for him to remember what he saw." And with that the old man sat down at the table, leaning back slightly in his chair, as a thin, rusty laugh escaped his throat.

The air in the room seemed to shift after that and they spent the rest of the night chatting away about hopes and dreams and how they both wished to get away from the castle some day. Jamie never spoke of the museum and Aldwin kept silent on the subject of his parents. It seemed that each of them was willing to give, but only so much. And as the night turned to day and the hard, familiar leather of the saddle dug into her backside once more, she fell asleep on the back of her trusted companion, arms wrapped firmly around his waist, as the stars turned to sunbeams in the heavens.

# Chapter 17

They reached the barn just as the sun was warming the small of their backs and as Aldwin trotted their tired but true horse into his respective stall; Jamie stirred, feeling the wetness from the small puddle of drool she had left on his shirt. A low groan vibrated on her lips as she realized they still had an entire day's work ahead of them. *That's what I get for going into the forest before the day of rest!*

Carefully, Aldwin helped her down from the sweaty animal and as she sat on a pile of hay in the corner, her eyes began to grow foggy as sleep pressed itself upon her. But a ferocious *bang* brought them both to attention as a figure in red hovered in the stall doorway. It was Lord Destrian and as he stood there, his black eyes burning holes through them, his large fist clenched angrily at his side, Jamie felt a wave of faintness wash over her, making her already tired head spin dangerously out of control.

Quickly, she tried to stand, but as the world went black before her eyes the last thing she remembered was the man with the angry, scarred face marching towards her, as Aldwin stepped between them. She awoke several hours later, when the sun had climbed high in the sky, leering down with a burning intensity. Slowly, she rose to her feet. The barn was eerily quiet. Even the horses stood as statues, as if they were aware of their impending doom.

Grasping the walls, Jamie inched her way along the barn, stumbling over clumps of hay and tiny rocks that had worked their way into the center of the floor. Everything still seemed a bit blurry, like she had been swimming underwater for a long time and had just come up for air. A thick layer of dry crust caked her mouth and as she ran her tongue along her teeth, a rough hand jerked her back, throwing her to the ground. Instinctively she curled up into a ball with her hands in front of her face, inching her way back with her legs that were spring—loaded, tucked into her chest.

"Get up," hissed a voice so evil that it made the hair on her arms stand up, "we need to talk!"

Backing away, Jamie leapt to her feet, her hands still blocking her face. The room began to spin but she steadied herself as she faced her attacker. Now was not the time for showing weakness.

It was the red knight, dressed in a matching shirt and pants suit made of crimson silk. A matching cape that looked as if it had been dipped in blood to achieve its deep color was draped from his shoulders. Jamie was forced to look away as the reflection of his shiny, black boots, seared her eyes. He was the picture of evil and as he moved towards her, rotting teeth exposed with a hateful sneer, she knew the worst was yet to come.

"You steal my finest blonk[14] and go gallivanting about in the woods at night? Who," he bellowed leaning down until his face was only an inch from hers, "do you think you are!"

Jamie shook her head as her mouth hung open in a desperate fear. Never before had she felt so threatened. True, she could escape this terrible situation when the moon was full again. But for now she was stuck with no hope of rescue as Aldwin had disappeared and the old man with the magic powers lived far away in the woods.

"Tell me," Lord Destrian said, pacing around her like a hungry lion stalking its prey, "where did you go, out there in the woods?"

She said nothing, her terrified eyes locked with his. There was no way she would speak of Dobromil and his mystical powers that lived in a house built by magic. He wouldn't believe her and if he did, what Aldwin said about being burned alive still rang loudly in her soul.

"Well, now there must be something of interest to you out there, something that lured you back night after night."

He knew everything, or so she thought. Lowering her head she silently admitted defeat. There was no point in keeping quiet anymore.

"Where's Aldwin?" Her courage was slowly returning. It was as if once she gave up hope, she could function once more.

---

[14] *large, powerful horse*

"Young Aldwin is with us no longer. He has been shipped away to a place where bad **theows** are sent. But he told me, before he left, that it was you who was responsible for this whole charade."

A fire burned in Jamie's gut as she lowered her hands, her back stiffening with resentment. *How could he sell me out like that! I thought he was my friend!*

"No, that's not true. I asked him to go but HE," she said, her words trembling with anger, "was the one who set up everything. I don't even know how to ride a horse by myself!"

The red knight nodded, scratching his chin as if he was hearing exactly what he expected. It was a shame, really. Jamie had been tricked because Aldwin, the only true friend she had, had been just that. Not a word had he spoken against her, taking all the blame for himself. The only reason the evil lord had bothered to ask her was to see if it was, in fact, true.

But it was too late and as tears of anger and hurt filled Jamie's eyes the red knight wrapped his arm around her shoulder in a show of mock sympathy. And the moment his fiery fingers sunk into her soft skin, she realized something was wrong. Unfortunately the grief and betrayal she felt silenced that little voice in her head that warned her of danger.

"Enough of that now," he said gruffly, pushing her to the side, "time to return to work. After all, my horses need to be washed and fed and I have a new shipment of hay coming in today that must be stacked properly."

"But who is going to help me?"

It was difficult enough completing the job with two people. Trying to do everything by herself would surely kill her. But the red knight seemed unconcerned. Gracefully he sauntered over to the entrance to the barn, his blood red cloak billowing out behind him. At the entrance stood a young boy, the same age as Aldwin, with wild eyes and matted hair that stood straight up on his head. Jamie stared, dumbfounded, as he was ushered into the barn and introduced as her new partner.

"He will assist with all the necessary chores. Now, get working!"

And with that, the manipulative master walked away, leaving the two of them alone in the barn. There was something strange about this boy and the longer Jamie studied him, standing in the heavy, awkward silence, the more apparent it became that she needed to do everything possible to protect herself. But, first things first; since he wasn't willing to be the first to speak she would break the tension.

"Hi. My name is Jamie." She said timidly, extending her hand.

He said nothing in return, his cold eyes burning in her chest as she stood with her hand out in the air. The seconds seemed like minutes and after awhile Jamie knew they were not destined to be friends. Aldwin had taken his sweet time warming up to her, but there was something different about him—a goodness that she sensed early on. Not so with this young man.

"Uh, maybe we should start by scrubbing down the horses. I'll wash this one," she announced, taking the sweaty horse they had ridden by the reigns, "and you can clean out the stall. That way, everything will work out in good time."

She smiled at him as she spoke, desperate to make a connection of some sort. If they were going to be working together they had to get along. With Aldwin, it was easy. He had shown her this method and as she thought back on their times together, her heart ached. But the boy did not return her smile.

"No," he growled, stepping in close, "I will stack the hay. Since you are a girl, you are weak, so you will do the dirty work while I do the lifting."

Jamie was shocked at what he said. Aldwin had never dared to speak to her that way. Suddenly she wondered if she had made a big mistake by telling the red knight everything she had. But it was too late now.

"But how can I do both?"

"After you wash the horse, keep him tied up while you clean the stall. Stupid girl," he muttered as he shouldered a bale of hay and walked up the ladder to the top of the loft to stack it.

Against her better judgment, Jamie stopped him in his tracks.

"Look," her voice was gentle and soothing, "there is an easier way to do all this. You see Aldwin and I—"

But he was not interested in hearing her method for an easier work load, mainly because it would be her that was doing all the work. Throwing down the heavy barrel of hay that landed inches from her feet he came lumbering down the ladder; face red, ready to fight.

"Now look here," he said, blowing his hot, stinky breath across her face, as he backed her into a corner, "I don't need advice from a girl on how to run a barn. I've been doing this longer than you, so just listen to what I say and no one gets hurt!"

"What?" Her pride drowned out the voice of reason that warned her to be silent.

He was really angry now, this wild—eyed boy. And as he raised his fist in front of her face, Jamie turned away, not wanting to take a punch head—on. But instead of hitting her, he grabbed the front of her dress, scrunching it up into a ball as he lifted her off the ground with one hand. Jamie's heart was racing at he pressed his face against hers, their noses crunched together as his brown eyes alive with fire.

"Don't you EVER question me again? You hear me, girl?"

He was shaking her so hard; it felt like her brains were turning to scrambled eggs. All she could do was nod yes as he tossed her to the ground and continued on with his work. The rest of the day was miserable and try as she might, she could not finish all her work. Lunch time came and went with the new boy gobbling up all the food in front of her while she watched, her belly burning, until she could steal a handful of grain when his back was turned.

A heavy weight was settling over her and when the evening finally came, she was just grateful to climb into a warm bed by the fire. But this bully would not tolerate such a thing and as she went to open the door to the run down cabin, he stood in front of her, blocking her way. His chest and shoulders were huge, bigger than Aldwin's and as tired as she was, she was in no hurry to get beaten to a pulp.

"This," he said, spewing the words at her, "is MY house. I live here, NOT you!"

And with that he walked inside, slamming the door behind him, leaving her out in the cold without even a blanket to keep her warm. Jamie spent the night in the barn, sleeping in the stall with the same horse they had been riding out to the woods. They had built up a bond of sorts and as she snuggled down into a patch of clean hay to keep warm, her thoughts returned to Aldwin, so gentle and strong, defensive of her in every way. How she missed him!

And as the night raged on she decided she was going to get him back. Even if he had lied to the red knight and told him it was her fault, she didn't care. They could work that out later. Dealing with this new boy was unbearable! Not only was she doing all the work, she was getting none of the food and was forced to sleep with the animals. A determination rose up within her and as the wind grew colder she began to formulate a plan to free them both. *The question was would it work?*

# Chapter 18

The next day went on the same as before, with the new boy dictating all the rules.

"Hurry up with those horses, or we'll never finish by the day's end!" He growled, sitting back to watch her on a stray barrel of hay.

With the hay having already been stacked from the night before, it gave him plenty of free time to sit around and critique her work. Propping up his dirty feet and letting a piece of yellow straw dangle out of the corner of his mouth, he conducted the running of the barn like an orchestra. It took everything Jamie had not to tell him to go jump in the lake, but as her mind returned to the violent shaking she received the day before, she thought better of it and kept quiet.

"You're not scrubbing them hard enough," it was the middle of the afternoon and after he had devoured their lunch there were no better time to take yet another break and watch her struggle with the horses and buckets of soapy water.

True, he had been generous enough to get the water for her, after an hour of pleading and attempted rationalization. Aldwin had always retrieved it before and he had never bothered to show her where he got it from. So, if the horses were to be cleaned the lazy bully was forced to get up from his comfortable seat and fetch the water.

Angrily he shoved the bucket into her chest, causing it to splash all over the front of her disheveled dress. The beautiful green dress that Aldwin had gotten for her was still locked away in the **cruck.** She wanted it back, but didn't know how to go about asking him for it. And looking around at what her life had become with piles of manure standing rank in rusty wheel barrels and feeling the dirty water and sweat drip down her back, soaking through to her underwear, she couldn't imagine when she would be wearing it next.

Finally, he closed his eyes and drifted off to sleep, letting a light snore escape his enormous nostrils. Jamie breathed a sigh of relief as she swiped a handful of grain to stave off her hunger and continued with her work. Her mind began to wander as she brushed down the sweaty animals, feeling the resistance of their taunt muscles under the coarse bristles of the brush. The long tail flicked back and forth as flies attempted to hover around their buttocks, swatting Jamie in the face. Shaking her head, she laughed out loud, only to have it cut short by the angry, red face staring directly at her from over the back of the animal.

Jamie gasped and dropped the brush, letting it clatter loudly to the floor. This awoke the sleeping bully who jumped to attention, chest out, back straight, as the red knight patrolled the barn. He had returned early for his next fresh horse and curious to see how they were getting along, had snuck in quietly to observe. Both were caught completely by surprise, with the young boy being the most embarrassed. With a red face he stood, staring straight ahead as the evil lord walked around him slowly, studying him from every angle.

Then without warning a tremendous *smack* was heard and the next thing Jamie saw was the boy fall to the ground, holding his face in agony. The knight had not yet removed his heavy gloves and chainmail which packed a powerful wallop. And as the terrified bully struggled to stand up the knight kicked him in the stomach with the metal toe of his boot. Jamie cringed as a painful wail arose from the young man's body, causing the horses to stomp their feet with nervous anticipation.

"You **sloomy** wretch! Is this what I give you food and shelter for; to lay on your back like a whore the entire day?"

He spat the words at him, as flicks of foam spewed from his twisted mouth, landing on the frightened boy's arm that was hovering protectively in front of his face. There was a fear in his eyes Jamie didn't know existed and as the angry lord closed in for the kill she knew she had to do something. True, it was enjoyable to see him get what was coming to him. But as the once powerful bully cowered in the corner, it reminded her that they were on the same side, struggling to stay alive against the evils of the red knight. Boldly she spoke, stepping forward from behind the horse, her eyes clear and steady, her fists clenched tightly at her side.

"He was helping me, milord. Only, he was taking a break when you came up."

The knight didn't turn around, but instead said his reply while staring down the young man in front of him.

"Is that so?" He sounded like a snake, hissing through fangs laced with venom as he spoke.

"Yes."

She had to clear her throat before she answered, fearful that the quivering in her voice would give her away. Slowly, the evil lord began to back away from the whimpering lad, never turning his back as he made his way over to where Jamie was standing. He didn't believe her, she knew that, but at least it would get him away for a while and then maybe they could become friends after all this.

"Do not," he sneered, pointing at the crumpled boy who was gradually rising to his feet, "let me catch you sleeping again or your bellytimber[15] delivery will cease for a month!"

And with that he stormed away, leaving them alone with their thoughts. Jamie approached the young man, extending her hand to help him. She truly thought this would be the beginning of a beautiful new friendship. After all, hadn't she and Aldwin gotten off to a rocky start?

But the bully was not interested in making friends, not with her. In fact he seemed angry and the reason as to why mystified Jamie. Hurriedly he jumped to his feet, slapping aside her arm, leaving a large welt near her wrist. The pain shot through her like lightening but before she could grab her hand back, he was upon her like a wild dog, snarling in her face, his eyes hot with rage.

"Don't you ever do that again," his voice was deeper than before and as he spoke his hand was slowly closing around her throat causing her to choke, as she was pushed against the stall door.

"I don't need the help of a woman, not now, not ever! Do you understand me?"

She couldn't respond, her face turning purple from lack of oxygen. All she could do was nod yes as the world around her became dark. The last thing she heard was the groaning of the door behind her, as he pressed her back harder against the wooden frame, feeling the splinters dig their way into her skin as he raked her down the post.

---

[15] *food*

When her eyes opened once more it was evening and with two horses still sweaty and waiting to be cleaned from that afternoon, she knew she was in trouble. The bully walked through the barn without looking at her, towards the shack she and Aldwin use to call home. In one arm he carried a cloth covered package and in another a sack of food that left an aroma behind that made her mouth water.

"See that you finish these animals. Don't want to be getting in trouble because of you."

And with that, he disappeared into the crumbling house without so much as a word of encouragement or thanks upon his lips. There was no doubt in Jamie's mind that food was for both of them. After all, it was she who had been seen working so diligently while he was caught napping in the corner.

Hot tears of frustration welled up in her eyes as she brought out the old, faithful horse which she and Aldwin use to ride in the woods together. For the past few days all she had been eating was animal feed while doing all the work. *And now this boy takes all the food and does nothing?* It just wasn't fair!

And as she began to prepare the animal for his rub down, the anger and fear and pain all came boiling to the surface, right there in the moonlight of the old barn. *The moon.* Slowly she turned her eyes towards the heavens searching for the one thing that would tell how much longer she had to endure this.

It stood bright and round in the sky, surrounded by a dozen twinkling stars. A few white clouds were scattered around, leaving eerie shadows on the ground below. It was getting fuller, but she could tell there was still a few day, maybe a week more before it would fill out completely. A smile curled her lips, dried from lack of water and sleep as she realized her time was almost over here. *In a week, I'll be back at the museum, back with Jimbo and all the statues and my own room in the attic!*

And after all that had occurred here, she wasn't sure she ever wanted to go on another adventure again. It was too painful, too draining on her young, confused mind. And it seemed to be getting her nowhere. *After all, what was going to happen once all the adventures were done? Where would she go then? Was she destined to spend the rest of her life in the museum attic?*

*No!* The word screamed loudly inside her tired head. She refused to give up. She would have her mother and father who would adopt and love her just as she was. She would be free of that orphanage if it killed her. And then her mind returned to Aldwin. To free him seemed to be an impossible task as she had no idea where he was or if he was even still alive. But there was one person who might know the answer to that.

"Come on old friend, lead me to the magical man in the woods," she whispered in the horse's ear as she climbed on top.

Jamie had not yet learned how to ride by herself, but after sitting on the back as Aldwin steered, she figured she could get the hang of it. She already knew how not to fall off and how to let her body ride with the rhythm of the horse. Getting a saddle on was impossible for her to do by herself, so she made due with reigns and an old feed sack that served as a blanket between her and the animal's sweaty back.

Carefully, she emerged from the barn on horseback, looking around for any prying eyes that might be watching her. The door to the shack was closed and a thin trail of smoke emerged from the chimney. Hopefully that meant the bully was tucked away inside, enjoying his dinner and the warmness of the fireplace, too content to go venturing out into the bitter cold of the night.

Another empty feed sack had been tied around her shoulders, sheltering her arms from the nippy air and another around her head like a scarf. Thankfully the young man had been too lazy to remove any of the old bags, which also helped to conceal her identity. Without a saddle she felt every movement of the animal as his legs moved back and forth causing her to shift forward slightly as she prepared to increase the speed.

Looking back over her shoulder the castle loomed dark, like a sleeping giant as she dug her heels into the side of the horse, urging him on. The animal went from a slow trot to a canter, which made her pitch forward, holding onto the reigns for dear life. Grabbing on to the mane it reminded her of the time she first arrived as a prisoner, ignorant and fearful. But now she was in charge and there was no one there to save her.

She remembered how Aldwin had positioned his body when the animal began to run and so she leaned forward, clenching the sides with her thighs, keeping her head and shoulders at an angle and forced herself to relax. In time her breathing returned and when she realized she would not fall off she began to enjoy herself, watching the trees zoom past in a green and brown blur, feeling the wind racing through her hair, whistling past her ears.

Fortunately she had paid attention when they were riding and so she knew the exact spot where the treeless circle was suppose to be. She reached it in no time, pulling back slowly on the reigns as the faithful horse slowed to a stop. Quickly she dismounted, falling into the dirt with a hearty *thud.* She was use to Aldwin being there to help her and never realized how difficult it could be getting on and off a horse by herself.

Cursing her own clumsiness, she regained her footing and holding tightly to the reigns, began to walk forward slowly. Jamie knew the game. The old man would appear to her and let her know where the house had been moved to and then she would follow him there. The minutes seemed like hours as she strained her nose for any hint of a smell that resembled baking bread.

At last she could stand it no longer and titling back her head she called out at the top of her voice, "Dobromil it is Jamie. Please, show yourself!"

The trees began to rustle with a deafening roar as a shower of leaves began to pour down upon her. There was something in the air and as the horse began to back away, his ears flat, she knew he had arrived. Shielding her eyes from the sharpness of the flying leaves, she felt a warming sensation as they twirled around her body like someone giving her a hug. And then they all began to swirl around and around, falling into a great big pile that reached as tall as the tree tops in front of her.

Titling back her head, while attempting to calm the horse, she watched as the leaves settled into a tower and then stopped moving as suddenly as they had started. Shaking her head, she turned away for a moment as a fantastic *boom* filled the air as a bolt of white hot lightening shot down from the sky and into the pile. Jamie screamed as she spun around to see the pile split in two with a flash so bright it blinded her.

The terrified horse reared, ripping the reigns out of her hands. With a yelp, Jamie clasped her hands to her chest as red blisters began to form. And before she knew what was happening, the animal was tearing away into the dark forest, leaving her all alone.

"Wait! Come back!" she called at the horse's retreating shadow.

But a soft *ahem* as if someone was clearing their throat behind her, caused her to turn around. There, in the middle of the pile, covered with leaves, was the hooded figure. His bony fingers extended to her, motioning for her to come closer.

"Come child," he said with a voice that cracked in rhythm with the branches of the surrounding trees, "the hour grows late and so are you."

# Chapter 19

The walls of the house surrounded Jamie like a warm hug as she sat across from the hooded stranger at the kitchen table; watching him scurry about as he set a pot to boil over the fireplace and placed a loaf of bread on the table in front of her. There was something about the familiarity that gave her comfort and even though she was absent her partner, it felt as if everything was going to be alright. He kept his back to her until the last possible minute when a steaming drink was delivered with gnarled, trembling hands.

She gulped it eagerly, knowing full well that if he wanted to hurt her, there was nothing she could do to stop him. The house had been closer to the circle this time, letting her tired legs which had stood all day and her back that was sore from bending and stooping, breathe a sigh of relief. A tingling sensation enveloped her body as the warm liquid coated her throat, coming to rest in the pit of her stomach. For a moment she wondered if she was going to pass out and wake up in the tiny shack once more.

And as silly as it seemed, she wished for it. It was short sighted to be sure, but the thought of waking up in the pile of hay near the fireplace with the thin blanket wrapped around her and a cup of fresh milk waiting on the table made her misty—eyed. And of course there was Aldwin, her only true friend and companion, an ally against the red knight. She could see him standing there as she unwrapped the clumsy paper package and basked in the reflective glow of his eyes as she modeled the dress for him, twirling round and around, giggling with delight.

"Thinking of a young man are you?"

The dreamy look on her face had given her away. And as she wiped away salty tears that stung the corners of her eyes, a knobby hand covered hers, squeezing ever so slightly. All that could be seen from the darkness of the hooded robe were his piercing blue eyes and as she stared back at him, a sense of comfort washed over her, making her weak in the knees.

"He's going to be alright you know."

The words took her by total surprise, causing Jamie to shoot straight up from her seat. All her emotions came rushing to the forefront but it took her a moment to compose herself before she asked the question that had been burning on her mind since the moment he disappeared that fateful day in the barn. With shaking hands she gripped the side of the table to steady herself, running quivering fingers through her tussled chestnut locks.

"Where—where is he? Is he okay? What happened?"

Blue eyes sparkled with mischievous delight before answering. His voice was calm and matter of fact. There was no indication he was lying.

"Closer than you think miss Jamie." This wasn't good enough.

"What do you mean, closer than I think? WHERE is he now?"

But the old man would not be rushed and as he titled his head back, draining the last bit of liquid from the cup, Jamie's patience began to wear thin.

"At the castle. He sleeps in the dungeon, guarded by ten men until his time comes."

Jamie's mouth flew open, her eyes wild with disbelief.

"But….how is that possible? The red knight said he sent him away!"

"The red knight said he sent him where all bad slaves go. That is the dungeon. After all, who would want to buy an unruly servant?"

There was a moment of awkward silence as Jamie digested what was just told to her. The hooded stranger took this opportunity to get up from the table and rinse out his cup in the sink. Alarm bells rang loud in her head as she replayed their conversation.

"What do you mean when his time comes? Are they going to kill Aldwin?"

The words caught in her throat as the situation suddenly became all too real for her. Up until now he was just a traitor who had been sent away; someone who made life easier for her but still did not deserve forgiveness for what he had done. This is what she told herself to keep from breaking down completely.

"He will be given a chance to redeem himself by ending the life of another and in so doing will earn back his rightful place at the red knight's side."

Jamie nodded to show that she understood even though a thousand questions were still whirling around in her head.

"Did you ever wonder," he said, returning to his seat in front of her, his back soaking up the warmth from the fire, "what they did to him in that castle the times he was not with you?"

She stared at him intensely, knowing something big was about to be revealed. Holding her breath she rested her chin on her folded hands that stood firmly under her chin. Outside, a lone owl hooted loudly, making the hair on her neck stand on end.

"Why is it you think that he was sore the next day and did not wish to be touched by anyone, not even you his only friend and companion?"

Jamie snorted in response.

"Some friend! He betrayed me and told Lord Destrian that I was the one who stole the horse and ran away into the woods!"

"Foolish girl," his voice was quick and cruel, "he would never betray you. It was all a trick by the red knight."

At this point Jamie could stand it no longer. Thick, hot tears were streaming down her pink cheeks as she choked back her shame. What hurt the most was that on some level, she knew it all along.

"He rots in a dungeon for you now. And so I ask you, young Jamie, what are you going to do about it?"

Sniffing back mucus and undescended tears, she whimpered, "but that's why I came to see you! You know all sorts of magic and stuff. Can't you do something to help?"

"For forty years I have lived as an outlaw in the forest, kept away from civilized society. They call me a witch. Claim that I conspire with the devil himself."

Jamie didn't know what this had to do with getting Aldwin back, but she was in no position to argue.

"After my wife died I began to practice my magic. When I was married, I kept it well hidden, so as not to burden her with the stigma that would soon be placed on me. For a while no one was any the wiser. But then," his voice grew dark as he stood and walked in front of the fire, "they came."

"Who?"

"The soldiers. Hunted me like a dog they did, chasing me on their horses, swatting at me with their swords. So I escaped into these woods and have lived quite contently here ever since."

"Can you ever go back?" She already knew the answer but thought it polite to ask anyways.

"Aha!" His laugh was stiff with knowing. "Do you have any idea what they would do if they got their hands on me?"

Jamie rocked her head back and forth. But he didn't even turn around to look at her. It was as if he was studying something in the flames. Slowly she got up from the table and went to join him in front of the fireplace. His withered hand waved above the flickering embers, making them dance back and forth. Squinting, she shook her head in disbelief as the image of a man on a horse ran across the shooting flames. He was followed by several other men on horseback, their hands raised high in the air, their bodies the same orange color as the fire.

Suddenly, there was a loud banging sound on the door followed by a ferocious voice that warned, "Come out you witch and face your fate! God help us if we have to come in there after you!"

Panic set in as Jamie shook the shoulder of the strangely quiet old man.

"They found us! How....but you have to hide!"

"No child. No more hiding. My destiny awaits me."

And with that he began to walk towards the front door. She followed him, pleading. *Was he crazy? Couldn't he just disappear in a pile of leaves like before?*

"Have no fear," he said turning towards her, "they are not after you and will let you walk away freely."

Jamie's mouth stayed open as she grabbed his arm in one last attempt to get him to reconsider. With Aldwin gone, he had been her last hope. The thought of him leaving too was more than she could bear.

"Open the door I say, or I'll burn this place down with you in it! Save me the trouble."

With a terrific sigh the old man turned and placed his hands on both sides of her head before leaning down to kiss her on the forehead. A slight twinge ran through her body like someone had just shocked her with electricity. And then he opened the door and stepped outside.

Two sets of hands dressed in black, leather gloves grabbed him and pulled him forward. Jamie hid under the table as a man dressed in a suit of armor entered the home, tearing through cabinets and upsetting the chairs. Finally, after throwing each cup to the ground with an angry grunt his beady eyes came to rest on the table under which she lay. *Oh no! He sees me!* She thought as he walked straight over, his body jingling.

But instead of saying anything the man reached down and flipped the entire table over, tossing it across the room. Jamie bowed her head, praying that he would not hurt her too badly. *But what of the red knight? What would he do when she was returned to him?* The thought made her sick as the man stood over her, heaving with rage.

And then, something strange happened. Instead of reaching down and grabbing her, he gave one last quick glance around the room before walking out the door. *Maybe he's going to get more men to hurt me.*

But instead she heard him bellow, "No, there's nothing else inside; checked it all top and bottom!"

She froze for a moment, uncertain if this was a trick or not. But after a few minutes she decided to get up and see for herself what was going on. It was better than being burned alive inside the house!

With much caution she approached the door and peeked out. The old man was standing in a circle surrounded by the knights on horseback, just like the ones in the fire. A lump grew in her throat as she walked outside and up to the circle, sticking her head between their bodies to have a better view of what was going on.

If they noticed her, they said nothing, all their attention focused on the old man who stood head bowed; shoulders slumped, awaiting his fate. The largest man was on the ground, dressed in head to toe armor that glistened in the moonlight. His fists were large and menacing looking and as he approached the stranger, Jamie's heart began to race uncontrollably.

"It seems," the large man gloated, "that we have caught you at last. Have you anything to say for yourself before you meet your destiny forged in fire?"

*No! They were going to burn him alive!* It was just as Aldwin said it would be with the exception of her being killed with him. A sudden dizzy spell overtook her as she grabbed onto a knight's belt to keep herself from falling over.

"You make kill me, but my magic will live on forever. That is one thing," the old man said with gusto, "that can never be wiped from the earth."

"Hey, who's pulling on my belt?"

The man Jamie had grabbed on to for support was looking around bewildered. At one point he look directly at her, or rather through her, confused. It was then she realized that the kiss given to her by the hooded stranger had granted her invisibility!

"Take him away!"

They were all so focused on the task at hand that the curious knight's question was ignored. And just before they loaded the stranger on to the wooden cart with an attached cage, the large knight pulled back the old man's hood as he spat angry words too faint for her to hear in his face. Jamie nearly fainted away when she saw who it was. The blue eyes and wispy white hair with a small "x" below his left eye was all too familiar. Jimbo!

Long after the soldiers had disappeared into the night carrying away the old man who was a stranger no more, she sat, unable to sleep at the fireplace inside the enchanted house. And as her eyes played tricks on her, making terrific shapes out of the roaring fire which turned to embers by morning she had made a decision about what to do. True, she had little information to go on, other than that Aldwin was still in the castle which she had no way to get to and that he would be able to redeem himself by killing someone else. *But who? And why? And most importantly, what could she do to stop all this?*

# **Chapter 20**

The sun beat down with a vengeance as Jamie dogged between the seats of would—be spectators, receiving angry swats to the face and some unwanted tweaks to her behind as she momentarily blocked their view. Heavy droplets of sweat stained her pink cheeks as she gasped for air under the flimsy canvas used for shade for the wealthier patrons. A young man with a canvas bag around his neck was serving turkey legs in white paper envelopes to any who could afford them. And as the greasy wrappers littered the ground she slipped alarmingly, nearly crashing in to an elderly woman in the back row.

It surprised Jamie that she was seated so far away from the festivities. Anyone who put that much effort into their appearance must have money to spare. Her long, gray hair was tightly braided in an intricate weaved design and pinned to the back of her head. A small gold hat with a matching veil encompassed her hair keeping it safe from any sort of wind that might blow through. Strands of long, gold and emerald necklaces were looped around her neck, dangling below her breasts which heaved under her impossibly tight dress.

Thick wrinkles formed on her forehead as she looked Jamie up and down before turning to her maid that stood next to her and said, "It's getting worse here every year. The daggle-tails[16] they let in here is simply abominable!"

The servant nodded in response her eyes never leaving the dusty field. And Jamie could see why. It was truly a spectacular lay—out, with brightly colored flags hanging from anything that was nailed down, fluttering like a young girl's eyelashes at her beau in the breeze. In some ways in resembled the other jousting tournament she had attended with the red knight and Aldwin, only this one was much larger and the people far more spectacular.

Silver ropes sectioned off the lanes that the jousters would be riding down and at the end of each station stood a peasant boy, dressed in silken threads by each jouster to show off his wealth and generosity to the crowd. The boys would earn their pricey garments, having to stand outside in the unforgiving heat the entire day, serving water to the knights and their horses and fetching heavy lances for them to stab each other with as they rode. And for some reason as

---

[16] *untidy woman*

Jamie stood watching everyone interact with each other, as the women giggled behind their hands to show how demure they were and the men laughing heartily while consuming massive amounts of ale, her eyes began to scan the grounds, searching for her friend.

It was foolish, she knew, to look for him here. He was probably miles away by now, or still locked up in the castle as Jimbo had told her. But this was her last hope. The red knight would not miss this tournament for the world as he had been training hard the entire time she had been there, almost a month. And who knows how long before that?

But even if he didn't bring Aldwin with him, there might be a chance that she could speak with him about her friend's condition. It was a long shot, but it was the only choice she had left. She couldn't go back to the castle after sneaking out at night and losing the horse. Otherwise, she would be sitting in the dungeon along side of him and where would that leave them? She needed something to barter with; something the red knight would want more than to keep Aldwin enslaved.

And as she ducked behind the wooden chairs, leaving behind the fickle crowd with their servants standing next to them, staring blankly ahead like obedient statues and into the sea of tents, determined swelled within her. It was not an easy choice to make but after thinking about how close they were to a full moon, she figured she would give herself to the red devil in exchange for Aldwin. After all, it was she that had stolen the horse all on her own and lost it somewhere in the forest and it was she who had defied him so openly be leaving at night with an animal that was not her own.

What she feared most was the beating. The way Aldwin conducted himself after staying in the castle overnight made her realize how awful it must be for those who disobey their masters. But strangely enough she didn't remember Aldwin doing anything that should be punished. And while she pondered this, her investigating led her into the first tent in the row. It was tall, with long poles reaching towards the sky and little blue flags waving from the top. Quietly she entered, peeking in through the canvas flaps first to be certain, before ducking inside.

The large, open circle of ground for a floor reminded her of their trips to the woods, causing her lip to quiver with emotion. It was dark except for the light from the candles that lined a small dressing table with a full length mirror that stood to the side. Pieces of shiny armor sat on boxes that lined the walls and empty mugs with a bucket of water stood next to the table.

There was nothing in the tent that indicated who owned it, as the armor stood bare of any coloring that would relate to a certain knight. Frustrated, she turned to leave as voices encircled the tent, causing a wave of panic to wash over her. Hurriedly, Jamie dove behind a cluster of boxes as the entrance flaps began to quiver and two men entered the room. They spoke in hushed voices, but their fear was evident.

"How can it be that a man who murders his own brother is free to ride in the tournament?"

These words were spoken by a tall, stately looking gentleman with wavy blond hair and dashing brown eyes.

"I don't know milord. Perhaps he knows someone in the higher ranks."

Realizing she was hidden in shadow, Jamie stuck her head out from around the box to see who was speaking.

"But the law is the law and yet somehow he is always treated with such, such, privilege!"

The young boy shook his head in agreement. He was obviously the servant of the dashing, older man who donned a white, ruffled shirt and handsomely stitched pants that tucked into knee—length boots. And even though his name was never spoken, Jamie knew who they were talking about.

"It should not be milord."

The man grumbled in response, protesting as he sat down at the dressing table to look at himself in the mirror. Reaching down, he picked up a thick bristled brush and ran it through his wavy locks. But there was something different about him. He was more than angry and as Jamie studied him, she realized his hands were trembling. *He was afraid!* Well, she couldn't blame him. The red knight scared her too.

"Come boy, it is time," he said, drawing himself up and lining his lips with sweet smelling oil, "dress me proper so that I may go out there and do our house proud against the forces of evil!"

The next few minutes were frightening as the servant moved along the boxes where Jamie hid, lifting up the armor and fastening it to the knight. At one point he dropped a piece, causing the knight to go into hysterics as he patiently fitted each section to his master's body. Finally, they were done. But before he would leave, the finicky man sat down in front of his dresser and began to powder his face. Jamie could barely contain her laughter as this seemingly rugged individual took such lengths to enhance his appearance. She had seen the red knight up close before and never witnessed a trace of make—up on his face. That was for ladies.

The only other time she had heard of men wearing make—up was at the circus. Granted, she had never been to one, but when it was in town posters were nailed to every tree, billboard and fencepost for miles around. She had managed to snag one when she snuck away from the playground one afternoon and went walking along the sidewalk in front of the orphanage.

It was so brightly colored and shiny with the picture of a funny—faced clown squirting water out of a flower on his jacket and an elephant balancing on a ball behind him. And at the very top of the flyer it said: *Come one, come all! Don't miss the greatest show on earth!* What sealed the deal for Jamie was the drawing of a little girl in the corner with a pink hair bow, eating cotton candy.

Later that evening when she thought she was alone, she studied the picture under the covers of her creaky bed. But moments after lying down, the blankets were ripped off her head and the flyer torn from her grasp by the curly—headed blond girl. She stared smugly at Jamie who struggled vainly to retrieve her picture.

"Hey, give that back!"

"Let's see now," the girl said, twirling a lock of her pale hair around her finger, "what could be so interesting that you have to look at it under the covers?"

The other gathered around, staring at the picture with oohs and ahhs of delight filling the room.

"Where did you get this?" asked the one with frizzy red hair and thick glasses.

"Is Miss Legree letting us go to the circus?"

"The circus! Oh boy!"

"Hey, give that to me! I want to see!" wined a smaller girl with crooked teeth.

And as the level of excitement grew in the room, so did the volume of their voices until the loud slapping sound of heavy leather shoes entered the room followed by the slamming of the door. Whenever she entered the room it seemed all the fun was sucked out with it. And as she glided across the floor heading for Jamie with her long, black dress trailing behind like a curtain, Jamie feared she would be swallowed up completely.

"What is the meaning of this? Is this the way for proper young ladies to behave?"

The sound of her voice reminded Jamie of someone stepping on a cat's tail with its shrill tone. Everyone got very quiet as the headmistress spoke. Some looked at the floor, other the ceiling but all, except Jamie, avoided eye contact.

"I cannot imagine what it is that got you all so riled up."

She scanned the room, her dark eyes resting on each frightened young girl, willing them to tell. No one said a word and for once, Jamie felt proud. It felt great to have them all on her side for a change. Or maybe it was because the picture was so pretty they all wanted another chance to look at it. Either way, it was a victory.

"It was this poster that Jamie brought."

Hissing through clenched teeth she turned her head to see who had ousted her. The pretty light haired girl stood with the picture hoisted high above her head for Miss Legree to see. *She might have known!*

No sound left her mouth as she took the flyer from the girl. Slowly, she turned it over, studying it carefully before speaking. Every vein in her neck stood out as she turned towards Jamie who was still sitting in her bed.

"Where did you get this?"

Crossing her arms in front of her chest, she pursed her lips in defiance as the old woman approached her bed. *There was no way that old bat was going to get her to talk!* But she didn't have to.

"I think she got it on the street."

Jamie's blood began to boil as her blond nemesis sealed her fate, smiling prettily all the while. She knew what was coming next and so she struck while there was still time. With blood pounding in her ears she jumped out of bed and grabbed the girl by the hair, slamming her head into the metal framed bed. There was a loud *thunk* followed by a high—pitched wail as the conniving child's head struck the bed, causing her to fall to the floor in agony.

And while her enemy lay curled up in the fetal position, Jamie was dragged off by her ear to the tiny closet in the back of the room. For the rest of the night she was forced to stand on her tip—toes, facing the wall. The next morning she was sick with a terrible sore throat from lack of sleep and cold. No one cared.

"All done now milord. It is time for you to ride."

The young servant held out the knight's helmet which was placed ever so gently over the freshly powered face. And then with a hearty pat on the shoulder and a few misguided words of encouragement, they were off. As soon as they had exited the tent Jamie followed, throwing herself into the midst of servants trailing after their masters in an attempt to find the red knight.

# Chapter 21

The earth seemed to move as the knights readied themselves for battle. The tournament had already begun with the king and queen sitting high above the crowd on a golden pedestal as two young servants waved large feathered fans to keep them cool. Their chubby fingers grasped sparkling wine goblets as peeled grapes were popped into their open mouths as they pawed the heavy trays laden with food, greedily. On the field, the jousting had fully commenced and as two unknown knights bravely charged each other, clashing angrily under the wicked sun, as the roar of the crowd echoed in clear sky.

In the meantime, Jamie had followed every servant she could find, begging for information.

"Please," she moaned, tugging at the tunic of a young squire carrying a pitcher of water, "you must tell me in which tent the red knight is!"

"Sorry milady," was always the answer, as they shook their heads and walked away at a quick pace to catch up to their respective knights, "the only tent I know is my own."

It seemed like she had been searching for hours and as the golden rays roasted the top of her head Jamie thought it best to rest, if only for a moment, under the awning of the largest tent in the back of the row. No flags flew above this one, but being that it was twice the size of the others, she figured whoever it belonged to must be important. No sooner had she settled herself behind the large flap for security, she heard a familiar voice pierce the air.

"Pick up the pace boy, or I'll send you back to the swamp from whence you came!"

A chill of fear and delight ran down Jamie's back as the pounding of footsteps against the soft earth moved closer. *It was him!* Waiting until she was certain they were both inside the tent, only then did she dare to peek around the corner to confirm who it was. There they stood in the center of the open air tent, the red knight slicking back his hair with a strange type of oil while the bully stood beside him, hanging on to his every word.

"Stand over there, don't stand so close," even when he was carrying on a normal conversation he barked his words. "No, do not bring yourself closer! It is the oil I desire!"

Jamie found a small tear in the flap which she placed her eye behind just in time to see the red devil smack the boy on the face. Normally it wouldn't have been so bad, except he was already wearing his thick metal gloves. And with one swat he sent the boy sailing backwards onto the hard floor as the oil he was holding flew up in the air and landed on his head.

"Look there, see what you've done! Acclumsid[17] child!"

The boy looked stunned, sitting there in the dirt, oil cascading down his head, dripping on to his shoulders. And as the knight loomed over him, waving his fist in anger, Jamie saw a look of sheer terror in his eyes. *He doesn't seem so big now*, she thought, remembering how scared she had been when he threw her up against the wall in the barn.

"For—for—forgive me, milord, I...." but the red knight had no time for apologizes.

"Why do you sit as if there is no work to be done? Is that what I pay you for?"

The bully shook his head back and forth, his eyes widening.

"Well then get up and help me dress!"

His voice filled the room, spilling out onto the row of tents outside. Several other knights began to peek outside, curious as to what was going on. Quickly Jamie checked to make certain she was completely hidden from view. The generous sized flap gave her ample room to hide herself, dragging the ground so even her feet would not show.

Inside the tent, the knight continued to give orders, shoving the boy when he did not move fast enough. When the time came for him to put on his armor, things went from bad to worse. He moved slowly as the red master called out for the different pieces of armor to be placed on his body in a certain order. His preferred method of dressing was from the shoulders down to his feet. But of course the boy did not know this. And as he scrambled around, grabbing random pieces from opposite sides of the tent, it became painfully clear that he had never dressed anyone in armor before.

---

[17] *clumsy*

"You aletude[18] little worm! How dare you not know how to dress a knight of my standing! And to be touched by such—such," the knight grabbed the bully's trembling hands, that were caked with dirt, "filth!"

Grumbling under his breath he began to pace back and forth, throwing wild hand gestures in the air as he considered the situation. At long last he tired and decided to rest his weary bones in front of the dressing mirror. A grand chair with plush, purple lining was waiting to catch his fiery backside as he collapsed, putting his head in his hands, bemoaning his fate.

"Of all times for something to go wrong, today!" He spat the words at no one and everyone, letting spit and undigested food chunks fly from his gaping mouth.

"The people are expecting a show. But how can I deliver when I am so drained?"

The young boy moved his weight back and forth, lifting one foot off the ground and then the other, the hot sand burning his sandaled feet.

"But you ride so well, milord." It was his only chance for redemption, a kiss ass compliment. And he took it.

"It's not the ride, boy. Everyone knows I can win this with my eyes closed. It's the show. But perhaps," he said, taking a long, hard look at himself in the shaky mirror, "killing that slave boy who betrayed me will bring some relief."

Jamie's head began to spin. *He couldn't be talking about Aldwin, could he? After all, who heard of slaves being killed at a jousting tournament?*

"You—you're going to kill him milord?"

"Not me you carked[19] ninny! I am going to offer him a chance to redeem himself by killing some old fool from the woods who is said to be a witch. And after he kills him, I will declare him a murder and slit his throat myself!"

---

[18] *fat*
[19] *anxious*

Jamie gasped audibly. *The whole thing was a trap!* She simply had to get to Aldwin before the red knight did.

"But what if he won't kill him?"

"What?"

"What if the slave won't kill the old man? What will you do then?"

The red devil snorted, slapping his knee with his hand. Slowly, he rose to his feet and faced the fearful lad. Placing his hand on his shoulder, he looked directly into his eyes as he spoke.

"Because he thinks if he kills the witch, I will let him return to me. To work and be back in my good graces. And what boy wouldn't want that?"

The bully nodded his head, but Jamie could see the doubt in his eyes. They continued to dress in silence, the sound of clanging metal echoing in the tent as sweaty hands carefully fitted each piece to his exact specifications. Everything was moving at a much slower pace which irritated the knight. He was use to Aldwin, who moved with lightning precision. And the bumbling of this clumsy fool irritated him to no end.

There was a long life of heartache ahead of this young boy who served the evil knight. Jamie did not envy him. She had managed to escape but she was not sure how much longer that would last once she revealed herself to Aldwin. He must have been hidden as if someone was looking for him, because Jamie had looked inside every tent and hadn't seen a trace of him. In fact, no one was talking about this little scheme except the red devil.

And then it hit her, *maybe no one else knows about it!* But why would he keep such a fantastic spectacle a secret? Maybe so he would look good in front of the king? After all, if someone else should get wind of it, they might attempt to upstage him later.

One hour later, after Jamie's legs began to shake from exhaustion and standing in one place for so long, they exited the tent. A sigh of relief swept over her as she ducked inside, searching for anything that would lead her to her friend. The room was cluttered with combs and various oils. Boxes lined the sides of the room labels like: jerky and dried fruit scratched on the side. There was nothing that she could see that would help her.

So, with a terrific sigh, she walked out of the tent and back along the row to get to the jousting tournament. At one point she considered going around behind the king and queen's pedestal but a troop of armed guards with sharp spears stood ready. Whatever was behind there was precious to risk public viewing. And with much angst, she left.

It pained her to think of Aldwin all locked up, starved, beaten, neglected. And like a wild animal in the roman arena, he would not be let in on what was happening until the last minute. They would need a plan of escape but looking around at all the knights in their shining armor and large, thundering horses, she knew that was difficult if not impossible.

Running on foot, even if they managed to clear the guards who would come rushing at a moment's notice, would only get them killed. The others had horses and she was certain neither she, nor Aldwin and certainly not Jimbo could outrun them. And so she began to study the arena, where the guards were the most numerous and where she thought they would present the prisoners. There was a tiny platform made of wood with a long beam that ran up the back. It was situated just below the king's pedestal and jutted out, giving the royalty an up close view of whatever would be happening.

Jamie didn't know how powerful the old man's magic was, or if he would be in any condition to use it. But she figured even at its weakest, they could make it out and back into the safety of the forest. And as the audience cheered and the jousters clashed together on the field, she made her way to the unguarded stables where a pack of fresh young stallions stood, nostrils flaring, waiting for action.

# **Chapter 22**

By the time Jamie returned to the jousting arena the crowd was in rare form. Apparently the last few matches had been disappointingly dull with little to no blood or injuries. They had been won by points which infuriated the blood thirsty mob who had paid good money to watch the festivities.

An elderly gentleman in the front row shook his head back and forth disapprovingly, his long, white beard fluttering in the wind. His suit was made of crushed velvet with hints of purple meaning he was part of the royal lineage. A long feather protruded from his floppy hat which reminded Jamie of a smaller version of what the cook wore in their orphanage. He wore a heavy lace shirt under a dark velvet coat and from the looks of his red face and blood shot eyes, Jamie knew he was in agony.

Everyone was wiping long trails of sweat from their faces with silken handkerchiefs and gulping from their silver goblets like a man crossing the desert who happened upon a bubbling spring. Women in their long, flowing gowns of green and blue keeled over in the sun, like wilted flowers, their faces long, their eyes tired. Jamie couldn't imagine wearing all that extra stuff. It just wasn't necessary, especially in the summertime. She had all she could handle in her green dress with the flouncy skirt. Never mind the layers of petticoats and ruffled undergarments they had on.

It had been a long shot, but she had managed to walk back to the castle, hiding out in the forest, just beyond their scope of vision. Surprisingly, it hadn't taken very long either, which seemed strange to Jamie, considering it took her horse at a full gallop so long to reach the old man's house in the middle of the woods. But what she didn't realize was that since his house moved by magic, it brought her closer to the castle while she was busy staring into the flames of the fireplace; too distracted to notice.

They were just about to leave when she arrived and she watched and waited for the perfect opportunity to strike. As soon as the bully left the hut and went into the barn Jamie ran at full speed until she reached her former home, out of breath and dripping with sweat. Quickly she entered noticing that everything was almost exactly as they had left it. The little chair in the corner in front of the stool—like table had been moved aside and the straw bed on which she had slept had been burned in place of firewood. Apparently this boy didn't know how to clean and bits of dried food and sticky, spilt milk lay all over the floor. His extra pair of clothes had been thrown over the chair in the corner and his pants hung over the dying embers of the fire.

Hurriedly she tore through the room, hoping and praying it was still there. Then, she found it, crumpled up in a pile on the dirty floor, hidden in the corner beside the table. A sigh of relief expelled from her lungs as she quickly put it on, tossing her old dress which was now nothing more than a pile of shredded rags, into the fireplace.

It was wrinkled and had some stains on it, but dear God it was an improvement! Happily she spun around, remembering when Aldwin had first given it to her and had asked her to turn around for him. Tears filled her eyes and a quivering found her lip as she thought about him, so kind and brave. She just *had* to get him back!

Sneaking out of the cabin she found the carriage the red knight planned on arriving in all decked out in red ribbons, flags and dabs of paint. Her first instinct was to hitch a ride on the back after the knight climbed inside and the bully sat upfront to drive the team of jet black horses that stood pawing the ground anxiously, red plumes extending from their bridles.

But another servant whom Jamie had never seen stood on the back and as they pulled away she knew there wasn't a moment to lose. Tearing into the stable she grabbed the faithful horse, who had apparently made it back to the castle all by himself, unharmed. Mounting him, she followed at a safe distance, not wishing to alert anyone of her plans. But after reaching the tournament grounds, she lost them in a sea of other fancy carriages that seemed to come out of nowhere, surrounding them like sharks at a feeding frenzy.

The trumpets sounded, alerting the audience to start of a new round. A collective groan was heard as people shifted uncomfortably in their seats, fanning themselves with intricately designed fans in an attempt to keep cool. Jamie positioned herself behind the back row, being careful to stand far enough away from the people sitting so as not to be notice and promptly removed.

She was out of her element here, amongst the snobby upper class. Their suspicious eyes looked her up and down as she did her best to look away and appear coy. Her usual reaction was one of attack and as they eyeballed her with such disdain it brought her back to life in the orphanage and the hatred and uncomfortable way they all treated her. They would rather she just not be there. It was as if looking at her reminded them of all the painful things of the world, what it could do to someone who wasn't very careful to tread lightly and do all that was asked while donning a brilliant smile.

But this wasn't about her and as the red knight entered the arena, waving diplomatically to the crowd, she focused her attention on the wooden stand in front of the king and queen. Everything seemed to be going swimmingly as he accepted roses tossed from the crowd and kissed the hands of fair maidens who approached, hiding their faces behind lace fans.  But then his opponent came trotting in to the ring and everything came to a standstill. The man's horse seemed twice as large as the red knight's and with its long, white mane and thick legs like tree trunks, Jamie could feel the fear in the devil's heart without ever seeing his face.

Causally, the knight entered on his snow white stallion, causing the audience to gasp and then murmur in sheer delight. It appeared as if there was going to be a real battle at last, one that promised blood, or possible dismemberment. Eagerly the people shifted forward in their seats, waiting with baited breath for it all to begin.

Jamie was so focused on the wooden platform she almost failed to notice the colors of the opposing rider. Decked out from head to toe in green, silk banners and delicate handkerchiefs he was the picture of grace and dignity. *It was **lord Crewe**, the green knight from the museum!* And the longer she studied his strides the more she remembered his gentle and caring demeanor that day she was captured by the red devil. He had tried to save her and conduct himself admirably. And as she leaned forward, thoroughly engrossed in the scene before her, she hoped, she prayed he would defeat Lord Destrian.

An elderly man entered the arena dressed in a velvet suit with matching stockings. His long mustache gave him an air of regality as he stood between the two ferocious men. Raising his hand high above his head, he spoke like a thunder God, his voice so deep it shook the very ground.

"Welcome gentlemen. I trust you will conduct yourselves in a respectable manner, for king, for country," the king nodded his head wisely as the man spoke, "and also for the dignity of your respective houses."

Both horses trotted back and forth, stamping the earth with their hooves and shaking their heads in defiance.

"You shall use your lances for glory this day, as the winner shall be given a seat at the king's round table and be considered for his personal guard. And now," he paused for effect, "is Lord Destrian at the ready?"

The red knight nodded his head.

"And lord Crewe, are you at the ready?"

The green knight bowed low in his saddle, acknowledging the man.

"Then," he said, his old voice wavering as he brought his hand down, "let the tournament commence!"

The next few minutes were a blur as the two knight slammed together on the field, stabbing each other with their respective lances. At the first pass, the red knight broke his lance against the green knight's armor, nearly unseating him from his horse. That seemed to wake the green knight who then came back with a vengeance, breaking not one, but two lances against the red devil, knocking his head back with a tremendous wallop. The impact was so great he was forced to take a short break to regain consciousness.

An announcement was made, shouted from the balcony by the king himself. He approached the edge, his royal robes of purple with a white fur trim cascading from his broad shoulders. Behind him the queen was fanned by two servants as she lay back in her seat, observing.

"Ladies and gentlemen it appears we have, for the first time today, a real fight!"

The crowd roared with delight. Women tossed their handkerchiefs high in the air. The men thrust their wine goblets above their heads, signaling their servants for more.

"Both men have fought bravely," he said gesturing to each man, "but only one can be at my round table. And so, it shall be said, that the next man to break the lance against the other shall be declared the winner!"

With that he sat down with the jeering audience singing his praises in the background. Both knights faced each other and were handed fresh lances by their slave boys. The green knight's servant was well dressed and obviously well fed with round cheeks and a healthy glow that radiated from his face. He looked up at his master adoringly and patted his arm as he handed him the lance. The red knight's servant reacted quite differently, sporting dirty clothes and sunken in cheeks. He looked away when he placed the lance in his master's hands, fearing his wrath and a swift beating if he did not.

The tension was at an all time high as the men faced each other, their animals snorting and sweating with anticipation. Most of the crowd were on their feet, making it nearly impossible for Jamie to see. Moving to the side she sat at an odd angle, praying for the best as the men began their reckless stampede.

Like two tornados on a path destined for destruction they collapsed into each other. A shattering of wooden splinters indicated that someone had broken their lance, but with the cloud of dust from the horses it was impossible to tell whose. The mob was on their feet, craning their necks around like demented swans, desperate to see something. Finally, the dust settled. At first all that could be seen was a man sitting on top of his horse with shiny armor that glimmered in the light. Only the top of his head was visible and with eyes strained Jamie could just barely make out the color: green!

A sigh of relief swept over her as she realized the green knight was the victor. And as the rest of the dirt gave way it revealed a most devastating scene. The red devil lay face down on the ground in a pool of blood. His helmet had long since been lost and as the bully rushed to his side and attempted to pick him up from the ground; the green knight approached the king to receive his honors.

"A good fight has been made this day. And a true victor has emerged. May you serve me and your country with the same honor and bravery that you showed on the field this very day.

Lord Crewe," the king said, leaning forward and pointing at him with a hand full of gold rings, "I hereby pronounce you guardian of the kingdom and my personal military advisor."

The deafening silence of the spell bound audience was broken as a cheer erupted, nearly giving Jamie a heart attack as the green knight was validated. Women wiped away tears from their eyes and men slapped each other on the back in a congratulatory fashion. But all this meant little to Jamie who was now wondering what would become of the prisoners Aldwin and Jimbo since the red knight had fallen.

A lump grew in her throat as she realized the loss of the red knight might have not been so great after all. And as her head fell to her chest, salty, unapologetic tears streamed down, leaving small, circular stains on her skirt. She was just going to have to accept the fact that she had failed.

But a grumbling throughout the crowd caught her attention and as the looks on the women's faces grew more harried, she was lured to her feet just in time to see the red devil, still battered and bruised but coherent, return to the field. Behind him were two men clasped in heavy irons, their clothes torn and dirty and their eyes downcast. Each man had a rope around his neck that the red knight was pulling on, dragging them through the mud when they didn't follow along fast enough.

Squinting her eyes hard, Jamie ran to the front of the crowd, standing off to the side so as not to be a nuisance. She couldn't see their faces but her heart skipped a beat as the evil knight yanked them up the winding stair case that led to the wooden platform positioned front of the king. The first man with a head full of white hair was tied to the thick beam at the back of the stage while the other younger, smaller one stood, watching obediently. They were too far away for her to make out exact details but she even with her eyes closed she knew who they were. Clutching her hand to her throat she mouthed their names silently as the red knight began to speak to the king. It was now or never.

# **Chapter 23**

"Your majesty," his voice was as terrible as she remembered, like fingernails down a chalk board, "may I present a gift to you and your illustrious audience; to show that although another man has bested me this day I harbor him no ill will and wish to show your graces how generous a lesser man can be."

The crowd murmured, whispering behind their sweaty hands as the bloody knight stood between them, motioning to the king and queen. The king appeared interested in spite of himself, leaning forward against the balcony as the queen glanced over the top of her fan with mild delight. Whatever he had in store grasped the audience's attention; an action which was much appreciated by the king who was forever looking to add more jesters to his court.

"You have my attention, Lord Destrian. Show us what gaieties you have in store."

Humbly he bowed before royalty, steadying himself as blood dripped from his head, staining the wooden platform. His armor was a wreck, dented and dirtied, smeared with a mixture of bloody mud. Sharp pieces of metal stuck out from his suit, making him look like a tin can that had been ripped open by a grizzly bear.

"Before you are two men of bad standing; the first being a former **theow** of mine, turned thief against his own master," the audience gasped as he pointed to the young man in a filthy tunic, eyes down cast at the edge of the stage.

"The next is called Dobromil, but you know him better as the witch of the woods!" Nervous laughter followed by anxious chatter filled the air as everyone looked back and forth, uncertain of what to expect.

"Now, under normal circumstances I would have the witch burned and the thief hanged as is customary in our land. But, if it would please our majesty, I propose a punishment of a different nature. Instead of hanging my servant of whom I have grown so fond," he swept his battered arm towards Aldwin, "I would forgive him and all past crimes if he were to kill the witch of the woods."

The king stood up, his glittering crown tilting forward as he spoke. "And what then, Lord Destrian? Surely the young man would be rewarded for his act of courage."

A smile broke across the red knight's face as he nodded his head. "Your eminence sees all. Of course! The young man would be given the one thing all slaves desire; to return to their master and work in their house as before, with no thought given to prior offenses."

The mob shook their heads in agreement. Everyone seemed to appreciate this noble act by the red devil. *If only they knew the truth!* And as the people spoke amongst themselves, Jamie took the opportunity to sneak down, past the rows of spectators, towards the entrance to the arena. There were no guards there now; as the jousting had ended and everyone was busy watching what was happening on stage.

Quietly, she opened the large wooden gate and peeked around. There was nothing but a large, open field in front of her with pieces of metal and wooden lance droppings scattered on the muddy ground. Long banners announcing the knights that were to joust lay flat along the walls. Taking a deep breath, she ran inside, hiding herself behind the brightly colored flaps of cloth, praying that no one saw her. She didn't need to worry. All focus was on the wooden stage as everyone waited to see what the young slave's decision would be.

"A very generous offer. You would do well to consider it young man," the king said, pointing at Aldwin with a fat finger of knowledge.

The red knight turned towards the dirty young man, his face covered with bruises, and thrust a short sword into his trembling hands.

"The choice is yours, young apprentice," he said, placing a hand on the lad's shoulder, "I would love for you to return to me, to serve me and my house and bear our name."

Sobs emerged from the fickle crowd as men and women alike dried their tears on their mud stained sleeves. It was such a touching show of heartfelt emotion. Too bad it wasn't real.

By this time Jamie had managed to position herself next to the staircase that led up to the stage. The banners were so long and the crowd so intrigued, she had shimmied along the wall, unnoticed. Pale, slender fingers pulled back the banner as she surveyed the set-up. She was waiting, for what she didn't know, as her heart pounded in her ears. In the meantime, the mob had turned from sympathetic to impatient as Aldwin stood, staring at the sword and then the old man, his mind racing.

"Kill him, kill, him, kill him," they chanted, waiving their fists high in the air.

The boy faced the old man and walked forward slowly, looking him directly in the eye. His hand felt heavy as he lifted the sword to his throat and held it there. Meanwhile, Jamie found her moment of courage and made a run for it, up the stair case and on to the stage as the audience chuckled in amusement.

"What is the meaning of this?"

The king, on the other hand, was not amused and called the red knight's attention to what was going on behind him. Curious, the knight spun around, his eyes wide with surprise at seeing Jamie's face. Her breaths came quicker as she approached Aldwin, her friend whom she barely recognized.

Lack of food and dehydration had done their toll on his once rounded face. His cheeks were gaunt and the sparkle had left his eyes. There was a faraway look he had that Jamie didn't quite recognize. He was a broken man.

Desperately, she lunged forward, pulling back his hand that held the sword. "No, don't do it," she yelled, her hazel eyes pleading, "He doesn't mean what he's saying to you!"

Aldwin turned towards her, his face ashen. He looked like a doll that was forever frozen in a plastic molding. Jamie's heart began to ache as she only then began to grasp what horrors he had endured to rob him of his humanity.

"Your highness, this is another **theow** of mine, a thief as well. It looks as though she has returned to rescue her partner."

"It seems, Lord Destrian, you have a habit of employing untrustworthy people in your household. This does not reflect well upon a man looking to advance his standing."

While this humiliating exchange was going on, Jamie had managed to pry the sword out of Aldwin's hand and get him to make eye contact with her. Grabbing him by the arms, she shook him violently, trying desperately to get him to understand what she was telling him. Tears filled her eyes as she begged him to listen.

"He won't free you if you kill the old man. I heard him tell the new stable boy that he was going to kill you anyways!"

"Is there any truth to what the young lady is saying?" The king addressed the red knight who was now quivering in his boots.

"Certainly not," he declared, throwing out his chin in defiance, "never would I attempt to betray you or this crowd. I am a man of honor!"

There was no response from her catatonic friend and in an act of frustration, Jamie took the sword and cut the old man's bonds, letting the ropes clatter loudly against the wood floor. A group of guards had gathered around the foot of the stage, ready to attack with a simple nod from the king.

His face was covered with a layer of filth and blood, but his blue eyes sparkled the same as always. Looking up at him, she smiled, happy that whatever had been done to him had not taken the same toll as they had on Aldwin. He was alert and ready. And they would need him at his best if they were to combat the forces of evil and win.

Reaching up, Jamie grabbed his bony shoulder and whispered, "How is your magic?"

The old man gave a weak smile. "Not as powerful as before. I need to live in nature. That is where I get my strength."

"Guards, seize them!"

The pounding of heavy footsteps shook the platform as a group of guards ran, in a single file line, up the stairs, directly at them. Jamie grabbed Aldwin's hand and interlocked her arm through the old man's. They were all going together or not at all.

"Can you get us to the horses, just outside that wall?" she asked, nodding towards the crumbling panel underneath the king's balcony.

A soft smile broke across the man's face as he winked, sending a single ball of burning light out of his tear duct, towards the top of her head. Jamie pulled Aldwin in closer as the three of them linked arms and the mystical man of the forest began to mumble an unknown chant as the guards neared the top of the stairs.

"Hurry, hurry," Jamie said under her breath as the guards ran on to the pedestal, surrounding them.

Tiny points jabbed into their backs as they drew their weapons. The metal sang as it was pulled from their sheaths, reflecting the sun light. She could feel the angry knights closing in, pushing their swords further into their backs.

Suddenly, the floor underneath them began to hum and vibrate, causing a stir within the group. The knights looked down, terrified to see the wooden plank shaking under their feet. They began to yell to each other, *was it an earthquake?*

The old man threw his head back as the pedestal rocked violently back and forth, throwing the knights to the ground. A few tried to hang on, but their fingers were shaken loose and they crashed to the ground, knocked unconscious by the blow. Jamie opened her eyes long enough to see a great, white wind spinning around them, like they were standing in the middle of a hurricane. Then there was a blinding flash of light.

When she opened her eyes once more they were standing next to a group of three, young stallions that were corralled by the gate. Jamie had carefully selected the strongest and the most virile looking horses for their ride. And they had better get moving fast. Whoever they belonged to would be missing them soon.

Without a word they mounted the animals and took off at break neck speed with Jamie hanging on for dear life. She was a natural on these creatures but was still scared of falling off, even with a powerful wizard on their side. Aldwin still had not responded, but had followed their lead and climbed aboard his horse willingly.

It seemed as if they were floating on air as the horse's feet barely touched the ground. Jamie enjoyed the feeling of the powerful muscles that flexed between her thighs as flecks of foam spewed from its mouth. They were together again, exactly as it should be. And somehow, in spite of the fear of getting caught and the pain of riding bareback, it made her smile.

The trees were a swirl of green and brown colors as they ran towards the familiar circle in the middle of the forest. From there, the old man would lead them to his tree house that seemed to follow him around. The cold wind stung Jamie's eyes as she squinting, putting her head down and letting the animal take control.

Soon enough they reached the circle and as they dismounted, angry shouts were heard in the background. They had been followed. But Jamie refused to give up hope. If they could just reach the tree house in time.....

Leaving their exhausted animals to graze, they followed the old man closely. Jamie held Aldwin's hand, leading him, uncertain of how he would react. The forest seemed darker than usual, even though it was the middle of the day. Thick webbed trees blocked all trace of sunlight, making it nearly impossible to walk without stumbling over a root or bush of some sort. Aldwin followed obediently and Jamie vowed to thank him properly should they make it out alive.

And at long last, they found it. Standing behind a group of thorn bushes with the inviting light of fireplace pouring through the open door, the tree house! Gasping with pleasure, Jamie ran forward, dodging the angry bushes that sought to hide the magical tree. Gleefully she stepped inside, inhaling the aroma of fresh baked bread, filling her nostrils until her stomach hurt.

Everything was exactly as it had been before. Smiling, she beckoned for Aldwin and the mystical old man to join her. But they stood, frozen, staring at something she could not see. Reluctantly, she left the warmth of the cozy home to see what was so captivating.

A reddish, orange glow illuminated the dark woods, casting large shadows all around. They looked like ferocious monsters reaching towards the sky, waving back and forth in the wind. A hard lump formed in her throat as she realized they were surrounded by the one enemy they never saw coming. Fire!

# **Chapter 24**

"Get in to the house, quickly!"

The old man shooed them inside the tiny tree house as the flames moved in closer. Jamie could feel the heat tingling against her skin even though the fire seemed so far away. It was like being swallowed up by a big mouth, slowly closing around them, ready to sink its teeth into them at any moment. Grabbing Aldwin's hand she pulled him after her as he stood, transfixed by the dancing flames. He froze in the doorway, but Jamie didn't stop. There wasn't time.

Hoof beats pounded the earth like an old woman making bread. It sounded like they were surrounded even though that would be impossible. The house would keep them safe—the house and the old man whose powers could protect. After sitting Aldwin down at the table, Jamie approached the old man, her friend, Jimbo. He seemed rather nervous, wringing his hands and mumbling incoherently to himself.

"What are we waiting for, let's go!"

She grabbed him by the arms and shook him gently to get him to focus. Blue eyes met hazel and a sinking feeling began to manifest in the pit of her stomach. Something was wrong.

His mouth puckered as if he wanted to say something, wanted to tell her the terrible truth but just couldn't bring himself to do it. Jamie didn't understand. *Didn't he have magical powers?*

And as the old man continued to pace around the house, Jamie grew more anxious. Looking out the window she saw that the fire was growing closer, roaring like a lion as it moved steadily forward. She could stand it no longer. The time was now for them to leave. Turning around she confronted the wizard, stamping her foot with frustration.

"What is going on? Why don't you just….beam us out of here or something like you did before?"

Shaking his head he looked deep into her troubled eyes as he with a voice that quivered like a feather in the wind, "I cannot miss Jamie."

Anger enveloped her body as tears streaked down her confused face. Mucus filled her nostrils as she turned her head, refusing to accept what she just heard. His elderly figure stood before her, not moving, as the table went in and out of focus through the salty film in her eyes.

"What do you mean you can't? You just did, just now at the jousting tournament!"

She stared at him, pleading, begging for him to try something—anything. They would be burned alive if he didn't come up with a plan. But from the look on his worried, cracked face, that read like a map of the world, that option was fading fast.

At long last he spoke, his words slow and thick like molasses.

"My powers are limited miss Jamie. They grow weak with age and time away from the forest. For you see it is the trees that give me magic. They provide oxygen and give life. That is what I draw upon. Last night I was taken away from my precious forest and had what little wizardry I still possessed—beaten out of me. At the tournament," he put his hands on her shoulders and stared sadly into her hopeful eyes, "I used the last of it."

Jamie's mouth flew open as he slowly turned and began to walk away.

"Well, well, when can you get some more—magic that is?"

"Not in time."

The words cut her like a knife, sinking deep into her chest. Clutching at her heart she walked to the corner and began to cry quietly. She had come so far, done a noble act by saving two of her friends and now she was going to die in the most horrible manner imaginable. Meanwhile, Aldwin seemed to have broken out of his trance and walked over to Jamie to try and comfort her.

Outside the impenetrable wall of fire raged inching its way closer. The sound of screaming animals as they ran for their lives, some leaving behind their babies in the frenzy sent shudders down Jamie's spine. Closing her eyes she sat down and let her forehead rest against the wall. She could feel the heat radiating through the thick wood, cooking a small circular pattern into her face. Aldwin sat behind her, rubbing her shoulders and whispering words of encouragement as the wizard continued to pace.

And then, something strange happened. The old man stopped walking back and forth and stood staring into the flickering flames of the fireplace. He seemed to be watching something and then when it was finished, nodded his head in approval.

"Well children," he said in a voice that rang with impish delight, "it looks like the hour is growing late. Let us all get some rest now."

Jamie and Aldwin turned away from the wall and watched in shock as the once forlorn old fellow began to dance about the room, clicking his heels with glee as he prepared two places to sleep in front of the hearth. They looked at each other and shrugged their shoulders. Who knew what that crazy old bat was up to?

"Come, come," he motioned for them to move over, "your beds are ready."

Aldwin was the first to get up, shuffling at a weak pace over to where the thin comforters had been laid out in front of the hearth. He stood there for a moment, uncertain of what action to take. But the smiling face of the peculiar old man convinced him. He lay down obediently and then raised his hand for Jamie to come and join him.

But Jamie was not as ready to accept what the wizard was telling them. All she could see was that they were surrounded by fire and going to sleep wasn't going to change that. Maybe he was hoping if they were unconscious, they wouldn't feel the flames eating away at their bodies. But surely that sort of pain would wake them up.

"What are you waiting for, young lady? Time stands still for no one."

"I—uh," she couldn't think of what to say.

And after all they had been through, there wasn't anything to say. He had no more magic left, no more tricks up his sleeve and yet, she trusted him. And if she was going to die, better to do it beside two friends than living a lifetime with a bunch of snotty girls in a cold, heartless orphanage who hated her. Resolve began to grow within her and with trembling legs; she joined them in front of the fireplace.

The forest had all but turned to ash around them and as the hours slowly passed, the stench of burning hair and tree bark began to choke the captain of the guards. Gritting his teeth, he spurred his horse onwards, determined to find the rebels. It would be dark soon but he was certain that if he waited a few minutes longer he could smoke them out. No one could withstand that type of heat and survive; so at the very least they would perish in the flames and rid the country of their treacherous ways.

Circling the wall of flames they had created for hours on end gave way to exhaustion and frustration. The men were tired of looking and seeing nothing but clouds of black smoke; not to mention the soot that lined their lungs from being in such close proximity to the blaze. Night time would be upon them soon and with it a whole new host of problems. Visibility would be nearly impossible as there were no lights in the forest, coupled with the pillars of black smoke that poured from the trees, clouding the sky.

"Alright men, let's keep looking. We will not rest, for king, for country, we must find them and bring them to justice!"

A muffled groan emerged from the group as they continued to circle the shrinking patch of woods. No one believed they were still alive, or if they were they wouldn't remain that way for long. A sumptuous feast was being thrown in honor of the day's events and to honor the new knight into the brotherhood. But instead of dining with fair damsels while lapping up expensive wine, they sat on tired horses, feeling a mixture of cold night winds and unbearable heat. It did not make for good morale.

"I—I can't sleep."

Jamie closed her eyes tight and tried to think of peaceful things like fairies with silvery wings, or sleeping on a billowy cloud with an angel playing harp music in the background. But nothing was working. The sounds of stampeding horses and screaming animals rang loud in her ears, distracting her.

The old man sat next to them, gazing into the flames of the hearth. He seemed very calm and resolute with a straight back and a soul-full expression on his wrinkled face. Jamie rolled over and poked him in the leg to get his attention. Whatever he had planned only seemed to work if they were asleep. And while Aldwin snored softly next to her, the worries and cares of the outside world kept her awake.

"Miss Jamie?"

"I can't sleep."

"I can see that." His voice sounded almost comical.

"Well, help me then!"

Clicking his tongue against the roof of his mouth he turned towards her and ran his hand over her eyes.

"Eyes asleep, eyes that are here, eyes that must rest, for the **full moon** to appear."

She felt the coarseness of his weathered hand brush over her face, tickling her eyelashes. A warming sensation began to wash over her body, starting with the top of her head and making its way down to her feet. It felt like someone had opened her up and was pouring hot chocolate in her veins. Smiling, she drifted off to a world of sailors and mermaids as she stood on the bow of a commanding ship, sailing the high seas.

A loud blaring alarm jarred her out of bed, causing her to gasp as a blast of cold air filled her lungs. Maybe the fire had gone out in the fireplace. She would have to tell the old wizard to start it up again, or risk freezing to death.

Carefully she sat up, wining at the crick in her neck and the stiffness in her arms. The room around her was dusty and dank, smelling of soiled clothes. Rubbing her eyes she looked around, her heart racing. *This wasn't the tree house!*

It took her a moment to remember that she was sleeping in a loft just over the museum. Her breaths came rapidly as salty tears stung her cheeks. Whatever her friend had managed to conjure, worked. With a grateful heart she climbed out of bed, noticing her ragged, brown dress issued by the orphanage was back on her body. It was a shame she couldn't keep that lovely green dress Aldwin had given her. It looked so much better than what she was wearing.

The light poured in through the overhead window, giving her a gauge on the time. Putting her ear to the ground she heard the faint muffle of people moving around underneath her. The museum must be open, signaling it was okay for her to leave her protective cubby.

After several tries she managed to open the hatch and, since there was no ladder, jump down. Her head still hazy, she stumbled out of the janitor's closet and on to the museum floor, making a bee line for the bathroom. She would need to look somewhat presentable or risk being sent away. Ten minutes later, after bathing in the sink and combing her hair with her fingers, she emerged.

Children of all ages and their patient parents crowded the floor, laughing and pointing. They seemed so happy and as Jamie's eager eyes scanned the room, she spotted her friend mopping up near the knight in shining armor display. He looked exactly as she had remembered, with the wispy white hair and gray jumpsuit. Smiling, she approached him, rapping him on the shoulder.

"Ah, miss Jamie, so lovely to see you today. I trust you slept well?"

She nodded giggling to herself as his blue eyes twinkled with mischievous intent. Reaching into his pocket, he pulled out a half—eaten sandwich and offered it to her. She accepted gratefully, wolfing it down in huge, hungry bites; peanut butter and jelly, her favorite.

And so engrossed was she in the wonderful taste of the food that flooded her hungry mouth that she failed to notice a quiet young boy approach from the rear. Timidly, he tugged on Jimbo's shirt and whispered something in his ear. The janitor nodded, patting the top of the lad's head.

"When you are finished there is someone I would like for you to meet."

Jamie licked the peanut butter from her fingers, shaking her head in acknowledgement. Any friend of Jimbo's was a friend of hers. A tall figure emerged from behind the old man, bowing his head as a sign of respect. Green eyes peered out from under heavy lashes and as their eyes met, he reached up and brushes aside his short, brown hair.

"Hello Miss Jamie. My grandfather has told me a lot about you."

She stood there, speechless, staring at that all too familiar face.

"This is my grandson, Theodore. He's visiting from the big city, London."

"If I'm not being too forward," the young man said, taking her hand and leading her aside, "I feel like we've met somewhere before."

A joyous bit of laughter escaped her throat as she squeezed his hand tight. They had been to hell and back together, battling with each other first, then the red knight, then the world. She would recognize him anywhere, no matter how he dressed. A suit and tie and a bit of hair cream couldn't hide who he really was. And although he went by another name, she would always remember him as an *old friend* who stood for her when no one else would. She would remember him as Aldwin.

www.ingramcontent.com/pod-product-compliance
Lightning Source LLC
Chambersburg PA
CBHW080902120626
46555CB00008B/2915